SEVEN SWANS A SWIMMING

Twelve Days of Christmas

Emily E K Murdoch

ARE YOU SIGNED UP FOR DRAGONBLADE'S BLOG?

You'll get the latest news and information on exclusive giveaways, exclusive excerpts, coming releases, sales, free books, cover reveals and more.

Check out our complete list of authors, too!

No spam, no junk. That's a promise!

Sign Up Here

www.dragonbladepublishing.com

Dearest Reader;

Thank you for your support of a small press. At Dragonblade Publishing, we strive to bring you the highest quality Historical Romance from some of the best authors in the business. Without your support, there is no 'us', so we sincerely hope you adore these stories and find some new favorite authors along the way.

Happy Reading!

CEO, Dragonblade Publishing

Additional Dragonblade books by Author Emily E K Murdoch

Twelve Days of Christmas
Twelve Drummers Drumming
Eleven Pipers Piping
Ten Lords a Leaping
Nine Ladies Dancing
Eight Maids a Milking
Seven Swans a Swimming
Six Geese a Laying

The De Petras Saga
The Misplaced Husband (Book 1)
The Impoverished Dowry (Book 2)
The Contrary Debutante (Book 3)
The Determined Mistress (Book 4)
The Convenient Engagement (Book 5)

The Governess Bureau Series
A Governess of Great Talents (Book 1)
A Governess of Discretion (Book 2)
A Governess of Many Languages (Book 3)
A Governess of Prodigious Skill (Book 4)
A Governess of Unusual Experience (Book 5)
A Governess of Wise Years (Book 6)
A Governess of No Fear (Novella)

Never The Bride Series
Always the Bridesmaid (Book 1)
Always the Chaperone (Book 2)
Always the Courtesan (Book 3)
Always the Best Friend (Book 4)
Always the Wallflower (Book 5)

Always the Bluestocking (Book 6)
Always the Rival (Book 7)
Always the Matchmaker (Book 8)
Always the Widow (Book 9)
Always the Rebel (Book 10)
Always the Mistress (Book 11)
Always the Second Choice (Book 12)
Always the Mistletoe (Novella)
Always the Reverend (Novella)

The Lyon's Den Series
Always the Lyon Tamer

Pirates of Britannia Series
Always the High Seas

De Wolfe Pack: The Series
Whirlwind with a Wolfe

Selina and Arthur and Dorothea
Caroline
Arabella
Sophia
Esther
Lucy
Jemima
London
Rupert and Frances
Joy
Harmony
William and Leonora
Olivia
Katarina
Isabella
Maria
Bath
Chalcroft
Fitzroy

CHAPTER ONE

Lthough there was no one in the coach rattling along the wintery road to see Arabella Fitzroy scowl, she did so anyway.

It was all so blasted unfair!

Glaring out of the window, which revealed a view of English countryside scattered with snow, Arabella sighed heavily and pulled her pelisse closer, her gloves gripping the warm woolen fabric.

It was most irritating, and the worst of it all was, she completely agreed with her father on principle. It was why they had had such a heated discussion that morning, as the final preparations for her journey had been made.

"I know you do not necessarily wish to go right at this moment," said Arthur Fitzroy, her father, a worried expression on his face.

They had spoken in the hallway of their London home, with shouts and orders being yelled around the place by the rest of the family. The house was in absolute uproar, but Arabella supposed that was what happened when most of the family was about to travel to Chalcroft, the seat of the Fitzroy family, and some were staying in London.

And she was being sent away in disgrace.

"You are not being sent away in disgrace, Arabella," her father said firmly as she voiced this opinion. "You have always known that your marriage would be arranged, I do not know why you are making such a fuss about it now."

"I am not making a fuss about it, the arranged marriage part, so much as being sent away at Christmas!" Arabella had protested.

That was the trouble with fathers, she thought with growing anger. She was not a child anymore, she was a woman past twenty years—she knew her own mind and was not afraid to let it show.

"Arranged marriage or not," she said as calmly as she could, trying to prevent her temper from rising, "you knew I had been looking forward to Christmas at Chalcroft for months—I want to see all our cousins!"

"Not everyone will be there," said her father as though that made a difference. "Sophia will be staying here, and Caroline—"

"Oh, Caroline and Sophia, they don't count," said Arabella as though her sisters did not matter. "You know what I mean! There are twelve of us Fitzroys, but six of them are our cousins, and I hardly ever get to see them anymore. Harmony is married, and I want to see Maria's new embroidered cushion, and the Christmas decorations at Chalcroft are—"

"Enough."

Arabella fell silent, though hot tears threatened to fall at any point.

She knew it sounded foolish, even to herself when she said it aloud. It was only a visit for a few days, and she would likely as not see her cousins at Easter. It was silly to be so upset about missing a visit when there was nothing stopping her from seeing them later.

But somehow being kept from them, while others were permitted to gather…it was most unfair. Arabella felt the injustice of it course through her veins, fueling the fiery temper that was forewarned with her scarlet red hair.

"Arabella," said her father slowly. "You are a woman now,

not a child, and I do not wish to have to explain to you just how important this match is. This marriage is."

Arabella hung her head. It was infuriating. Why was it that fathers were always so downright reasonable when she wanted to shout and scream and rail at the world?

Her older sisters, Jemima and Caroline, had married for love. No one had expected their matches, and in some ways, though it had been almost two years since their weddings, the Fitzroy family were still getting accustomed to them.

Hugh was a dear old thing, at least in Arabella's opinion, while her sisters Esther and Lucy preferred Stuart. They would. It was difficult not to prefer an earl.

It was only the youngest Fitzroy of London, Sophia, who had openly said she had no preference.

None of Arabella's sisters had passed comment on her betrothed of course, and that was because they had never met him. None of them had.

"I know this marriage is important to you, Papa," Arabella said with a sigh. "It's just—"

"Watch out!"

Both Arabella and her father leapt back as a trunk, half tied up with brown string, clattered down the staircase and fell open at the bottom, spraying gifts wrapped in brown paper across the floor.

"It always does that," said Esther with a groan as she followed it down the stairs. "No matter what I do to it, the thing just keep bursting open!"

"Do you not think you are trying to pack too much into it?" asked Arabella with a grin as she leaned forward to help put the gifts back inside. "Goodness, are you sure you aren't moving to Chalcroft?"

Esther giggled. "As though Uncle William would permit such a thing! He's got enough on his hands with his four!"

The two sisters laughed, and their father sighed with a shake of his head. "My older brother loves company, do not even jest about it—if he could tempt all the Fitzroy cousins to stay at Chalcroft all year round, you know he would!"

Arabella smiled as she placed the last few gifts in the trunk. She knew she should feel grateful to have the family that she did, really. There could not be many brothers like her father her two uncles, who actually liked each other.

Uncle William lived in the family seat, Chalcroft, while Uncle Rupert had a beautiful townhouse in Bath—Esther and Lucy had stayed there a few years ago, and Arabella had the past summer.

Her father and her five sisters—well, not Jemima and Caroline now, of course—lived in London, yet despite the distance between the cousins, the Fitzroys were able to often meet together and indulge in familial gossip, high spirits, and laughter.

It was why she was so unhappy with being excluded this year.

"Are you not packed, Arabella?" asked Esther innocently as she tried to sit on the lid of her trunk. "I saw your trunk on your bed, completely empty!"

No matter what Arabella did, she could not catch her sister's eye to make her keep quiet. She turned to her father with a rather sheepish grin.

"Arabella Fitzroy, do you mean to tell me that you are not even packed yet?"

"Well, I thought," said Arabella hastily, glaring at Esther, who had the goodness to look a little embarrassed, "thought you might change your mind, Papa, and permit me to come to Chalcroft and celebrate Christmas with the rest of the family, and—"

"Absolutely not," said their father sternly. "Arabella, you knew this day was coming. It cannot be a surprise to you that now you are a lady, it is time to take your responsibilities seriously."

Arabella glowered.

"I think I'll just see how Lucy is getting on," said Esther in a falsely bright voice. "Have a wonderful time at...well. Have a lovely Christmas, Bels."

Kissing her sister swiftly on the cheek, Esther rushed upstairs in a medley of shouts to Lucy and Sophia, giggling as she raced along the corridor.

Arabella sighed heavily and dropped onto the lid of the trunk that Esther had been trying so hard to close. It snapped shut with a loud click.

"I just...I do not think I have ever spent a Christmas away from you, Papa," Arabella said quietly. "Not any of you. The idea of having a Christmas Day without any of my family, none of our traditions—I do not even know what they eat on Christmas Day!"

The tears that had threatened to fall for so long now did so. A few drops splattered onto her gown before Arabella was able to brush them away furiously.

And she was furious at herself. She had known for years, almost as long as she could remember, that she would be marrying Lord Nathaniel Cartier. His father was her father's best friend. The match had been made almost when they were in their cradles.

The fact she had never met Lord Nathaniel was neither here nor there. Arabella knew her duty, had known it forever. She had never attended a ball and made eyes at a young gentleman or wondered why a specific man did not ask her to dance or wish that a certain someone would attend a card party or walk her around the room or anything like that.

She had always known, always believed herself to be set apart. Apart from her sisters, apart from all other gentlemen, because there was one already marked out for her.

Lord Nathaniel. She had no idea what he was like, though her imagination had played many a trick on her in the past.

"Arabella, I am not sending you away to be punished," said her father softly as he sat down on the trunk beside her. "It is true, Christmas will not quite be the same without you—but I do this for your happiness, though you may find that a little hard to believe."

Arabella glanced at her father. "You...you are?"

Her Papa nodded, sighing heavily. "You are to marry this man, and in truth, though I have had doubts about it in the past, I still believe I ought to keep to my word…but that's neither here nor there. When you marry Lord Nathaniel, you will be his wife. I have been fortunate enough in my time to have two marriages, and I tell you now. a marriage is always better with keen understanding between husband and wife."

Arabella nodded. She could hardly refute such words; they were laden with truth and honesty.

"I know, it's just—"

"Arthur!" Selina Fitzroy, Arabella's mother, almost tripped into the hallway, so great was her haste to be moving. "Arthur, it's coming!"

Arabella's Papa blinked at her. "Coming?"

"Make haste, make haste—Mrs. Bird, call the carriage, linens, we need linens!" Selina shouted along the corridor, as though their housekeeper may not hear them unless she screamed at the top of her lungs. "It's coming, you dear man, now move!"

"Move?" repeated Arthur, utterly at a loss. "What?"

Arabella could not help but laugh. Well, they had all waited so long, it was no wonder that her father had forgotten Caroline's…condition.

"Caroline's baby, Papa," she sent gently, nudging her father to his feet. "You have remembered that you are about to be a grandfather, have you not?"

"Oh, a grandmother, at my age!" said Selina, bursting into tears. "My baby! My baby's baby!"

"Yes, right, well. A baby," said Arthur, evidently unsure precisely what he should be doing in that moment and consoled himself by taking his sobbing wife into his arms. "My dear, you must hurry!"

"I must? I must!"

Arabella smiled affectionately as she looked at her parents, almost beside themselves with excitement and worry. Caroline's baby. Well, they had expected it for a few weeks now, and it was finally here. At least, almost. A little Walsingham. Perhaps an heir to the earldom.

It was such a picture of happiness that it made her stomach squirm slightly.

Was this her future? Her parents had married for love; at least, that was what they had always told their daughters, and Arabella had no reason to doubt them. It was not common, of course, a pure love match—but then Arthur Fitzroy, despite being the youngest of his brothers, had plenty of fortune to support a family.

And she had been matched. Lord Nathaniel Cartier had been destined to be her husband since she had been born.

But would they find this sort of comfort with each other? This kind of affection?

As Arabella watched her father dry the eyes of her mother with his kisses, his murmured jesting making her laugh, Arabella's stomach tightened painfully.

Surely not. That was the true affection that a love match could bring.

She would be fortunate indeed if she admired or even respected her husband, she knew that. How many of their acquaintances in London absolutely loathed their partners?

And that was why, she saw with a sinking feeling, her Papa was so determined for her to go and visit the Cartiers this Christmas. A chance to get to know them. An opportunity to see them as they were, as a family.

The family that she would one day be joining, and perhaps not too distantly in the future.

"No, no, you should still go to Chalcroft," Selina was saying to her husband. "No offense, my dear, but I do not believe you will be much help."

Arabella giggled, and her parents turned to look at her, as though they had entirely forgotten she was there.

"Arabella," said her Papa. "Go and pack. Now."

She knew better than to argue. And that was why, several

hours later, Arabella found herself alone in a freezing cold carriage, on the road to Sussex, where the Cartiers' home was.

A ray of sunlight broke into the carriage, pouring light onto her face, and much desired warmth. Arabella closed her eyes for a moment, letting its amber glow seep through her eyelashes.

Well, so what if the rest of the Fitzroy family—save her mother and Sophia, who had rushed off to be with Caroline—were going to Chalcroft to be merry? So what if they would have larks she could not participate in?

Arabella had even heard murmurings from Jemima, who had rushed in at the last minute before she had left for Sussex, that she had guessed there would be a Christmas ball.

"Uncle William loves balls," Jemima had said confidently, her husband, Hugh's, arm around her shoulders protectively, though against what, Arabella could not tell. "A Christmas ball!"

A ball! Arabella sighed and sunk lower in the carriage as it rattled along the frozen road. A Christmas ball at Chalcroft, the beautiful manor house that seemed perfectly designed to host such a gathering.

And she was on her way to Oxcaster Lacey, alone, to spend the Christmas season with Lord Nathaniel and his parents.

Arabella sighed heavily, watching her breath blossom out before her. An arranged marriage was all very well, but the name Lord Nathaniel Cartier did not exactly stir up feelings of warmth.

Only once had Arabella seen anything of Lord Nathaniel. When she had turned eighteen, amongst the many presents that she had received from her caring friends and relations had been an elegant profile silhouette.

"Who on earth could that be?" Jemima had asked, snatching it away from Arabella's hands the moment she had opened it.

"Well, I might be able to tell you if I have more than a second to look at it!" Arabella had laughed, taking it from her sister's hands.

Seated in the carriage on the way to meet him, Arabella drew out the silhouette from her reticle. It was small, perhaps three or four inches across, and showed the haughty profile of a gentleman.

That was all one could make out, really. The silhouette did not show a great amount of detail, which may have been because it was roughly made, or because the sitter himself did not have many defining features.

Arabella sighed, placed it back in her reticule, and leaned back in the carriage. Perhaps he would astound her with his brilliance, with his kindness, his goodness.

Perhaps he would be remarkably handsome. Her sisters' husbands were all very well, but they were certainly not to her taste. She wanted something…well. A bit more interesting. A bit more dashing.

A cavalier sort of gentleman, Arabella thought dreamily as she allowed her imagination to carry her away. A man with great looks, great talents, but a haughty expression. A man who would debate with her, but always in the end acquiesce to her good taste.

And most importantly, and she flushed to think it, even to herself in the privacy of her own carriage, a gentleman that made her feel warm. That made her want to receive his kisses, his embraces.

A man she would want to—

"Here we are, Miss Arabella."

Arabella started. For a moment, she had almost forgotten where she was, in a carriage bound for Oxcaster Lacey to meet with her future husband.

Her coachman grinned down at her. "And a beautiful place it is, too, if you ask me."

Arabella moved to the window, looking out of it eagerly.

The carriage was slowing now as it trundled along a very elegant driveway lined with huge oak trees, empty of their leaves at this time of year but would doubtlessly be impressive and imposing in the summer.

To her left was a large woodland, or parkland. If Arabella

looked closely…was that deer just on the edge of the woodland?

But that was not the most impressive part of the view. Moving to the window on the right-hand side, she gasped to see the most spectacular lake she had ever seen in her life. It appeared to go on and on forever, with no break, cresting around a hill. There were birds everywhere, chattering and squawking, making the most delightful noises, and in one corner there were swans.

Swans. Arabella smiled at the soft, majestic whiteness of them as the carriage passed by slowly. The larger ones ruffled their feathers at her as the carriage went by, then returned to grooming.

"And there's the house."

The coachman's words were spoken in awe, but from this angle, Arabella could not yet see the place. Only when the drive curved to the right, to follow the line of the lake, did her mouth fall open.

She had thought Chalcroft impressive, but this? This was incomparable. The tall manor house was built in the Tudor style, all red brick and curly chimneys from which white smoke was billowing. There were oriel windows above, and from what Arabella could see from the carriage, festoons of holly draped below each window.

Arabella swallowed as the carriage came to a gentle stop outside the manor. Her heart was thundering now, thundering painfully against her chest.

This was not what she had expected. Her father had never given her to understand that the Cartiers were this magnificent! And she had only brought three gowns with her!

A swan lake, a deer park, and a beautiful house that looked as though it had weathered many a storm without a single tile being taken from its roof. For a Fitzroy who lived in a beautiful, albeit cramped, terrace house in London, this was far from home indeed.

Not for the first time, Arabella wished she had been able to prevail upon one of her sisters to accompany her—but they had been, naturally, far more interested in a Christmas at Chalcroft with the rest of the family than visiting a family they had never met before.

Stomach twisting, knowing that she could not stay in the carriage forever, Arabella took a deep breath.

The carriage door opened, and her coachman's hand appeared to assist her down. "Ready, Miss Arabella?"

It was only another family, Arabella told herself firmly, as her breath caught in her lungs. *Just a family with a son. A son who will become your husband. That is all.*

Arabella leaned forward and took her coachman's hand. "I am ready."

CHAPTER TWO

ARABELLA BLINKED AGAINST what felt like the harshness of the sunlight as she stepped onto the driveway of Oxcaster Lacey.

Well, she was here. She had finally made it. She was about to meet the family she would soon become a part of.

It appeared that she had gripped the hand of her coachman a little too hard, however, as he helped her to descend from the carriage.

"Argh!"

"I am sorry," Arabella said hastily, heat blossoming over her cheeks. It was only because she was nervous, she told herself, and it was perfectly natural to feel nervous.

She was about to meet her future husband. She was about to meet the person on whom all her happiness would depend.

A horrible lurch rushed through her stomach as a rather unpleasant thought struck her.

Arabella had spent most of the journey in the carriage dreaming up what her future husband, Lord Nathaniel Cartier, could look like, be like, what he sounded like…perhaps what he kissed like.

All her thoughts had been focused on him, and whether he would please her.

But what if he was disappointed in her? Arabella swallowed

and tried to push the thought from her mind, but it was almost impossible.

What if he did not think her pretty enough? What if he looked at her and was disheartened by the idea that he would have to spend the rest of his life with her?

It was a terrible thought. For the first time since she had left London, Arabella wished she had spent a little more time thinking about her apparel and her toilette. She had not even done anything interesting with her hair, merely pinned it up and shoved her favorite winter bonnet on.

Arabella looked down. Her pelisse was elegant, it was true, but there was little style in it. Her red hair was a little too vibrant to be fashionable, and her nose—well, the less said about her nose the better.

Flutterings of panic washed through her heart. What if Nathaniel—Lord Nathaniel, she must remember to address him properly—was utterly delightful, handsome to boot, but he decided that she was not sufficiently pretty or witty enough to be his wife?

Arabella swallowed. That was the difficulty with being one of six sisters, she thought darkly as the coachman released himself from her grip and started back to the carriage, wringing his hand, to retrieve her luggage.

There was always a Fitzroy to compare oneself to. Harmony was musical, and Joy was witty, her two Bath cousins. The Chalcroft cousins had all the nobility the seat gave them and were charmingly beautiful, their Italian mother giving them hot tempers but also passionate souls.

Her own sisters were equal parts kind and pleasant to be around, each of them with their own unique quirks that made them such popular guests.

And then…Arabella.

She smiled weakly up at the imposing Tudor manor before her. It felt much larger, now that she was standing here looking at it. Frightening. Almost overwhelming.

Perhaps it was not too late to get back into the carriage and simply drive back to London. The thought struck Arabella and appeared instantly to be a good one. Why, no one had come out yet to greet them, it was more than possible that no one had seen her arrive.

All she had to do was get back into the carriage, and—

"Ah, Miss Fitzroy!"

Arabella winced, carefully rearranged her face into a smile, and turned around. "Lady Cartier."

The older woman, still very beautiful and elegant, though her hair was silver, beamed. "I thought I heard the carriage! How wonderful to finally meet you, we have heard such wonderful things about you from your father."

Arabella smiled weakly. Why was it that whenever someone said that they had heard wonderful things about her, she was immediately filled with a sense of panic?

It was surely kindly meant. Lady Cartier looked like a pleasant woman, and she had done Arabella a great honor by coming out to meet her herself, not leaving it to a butler or housekeeper—but still.

It was strange, to think that her father had been writing to Lord and Lady Cartier about her as though she was a prize specimen at a fair, just waiting to be chosen as the winner for their son's affections.

"Why, thank you, Lady Cartier," she managed to say after an awkward moment of silence. "It is truly an honor to be invited to stay with you for the Christmas season. I…I am sure we will have a wonderful time."

Was it Arabella's imagination, or did a flicker of concern pass over her hostess's face?

If it did, it was gone in an instant. Lady Cartier beamed. "It is our pleasure, my dear—I say our pleasure, I did tell my husband that you were—ah, here he is."

A tall, rather imposing man—not unlike his house—came down the steps in heavy footsteps and examined Arabella.

"Arabella Fitzroy," he said in a deep voice.

It was all Arabella could do not to smile, though she was not entirely sure if she was supposed to. Lord Cartier was rather an imposing figure in her imagination, always had been, from the moment Arabella had been made to understand as a small girl that one day she would leave her father's house—not like this, for Christmas, but permanently—and come to live with another family.

But now she was meeting Lord and Lady Cartier, Arabella had to admit to herself that they looked…well, ordinary. Very stylish, of course, and with money. One could see that in the necklace Lady Cartier was wearing, and the way they held themselves.

But just people.

Arabella let out the air she had held for far too. "Lord Cartier."

The man cracked a smile. "And I suppose you are here to inspect the goods."

"Cartier!"

Arabella chuckled as Lady Cartier whacked her husband on the arm.

"That is no way to speak to your future daughter-in-law," Lady Cartier scolded. "If you are not careful, she will take against you and decide to leave without—well. Anyway, Miss Fitzroy, your man can take your things inside, we have set aside a suite for you in the west wing."

Laughter gone, Arabella swallowed but could think of nothing to say, so nodded.

A suite? The west wing? Just how large was this house, anyway?

"That…that is very kind of you," said Arabella awkwardly.

Well, what else could she say? It was in moments like these that she dearly wished she had been more able to persuade a few, or just one, of her sisters to accompany her. Why couldn't Sophia, considered too young to go to Chalcroft for Christmas, have accompanied her?

"Because if she is too young for family, she is too young for strangers," their mother had said firmly when Arabella had asked her.

Arabella has seen the sense of her mother's answer, but still. It did not make this any easier. If only she had someone who could stand by her side, support her, guide her where necessary to say the right things.

Her heart contracted painfully. Like a husband. Where was Nathaniel?

"Where is Nathaniel?" asked Lord Cartier, as though he heard Arabella's thoughts. "I thought he would be here?"

"I sent a servant to find him," said Lady Cartier under her breath while holding a smile for Arabella. "I am sure he will be here any moment."

The three of them stood outside the Oxcaster Lacey for almost a full minute, Arabella's heart racing. So, it was now, here, that she would meet him. The man who she would learn, she hoped, to love.

If only she could fall in love at first sight. It was a foolish notion that one of her cousins, Katarina, had always laughed at, but Arabella had always secretly hoped it would be possible for her.

What could be more romantic than being engaged to a gentleman one's entire life, she had always thought, and then when one finally met him, discovering he was all one's heart desired anyway?

Arabella swallowed. There were footsteps coming up the drive behind her; footsteps that were far heavier than her coachman's—and besides, he was taking her trunk upstairs to this new suite of hers.

And so that had to mean...

"Ah, Nathaniel," said Lady Cartier brightly—a little too brightly, Arabella noticed. "There you are. Miss Arabella Fitzroy has just arrived."

Arabella hesitated for a moment before she turned around, trying to take a deep, calming breath. She was suddenly very aware of her fingers, her hands hanging down by her sides.

This was it. She would turn around in just a moment and see the handsome, charming man that she had been waiting for her entire life.

Arabella turned around, her heels digging into the gravel, and she saw…

Her mouth fell open. If she had not just heard Lady Cartier address the man who was walking toward her as Nathaniel, she would never have been able to guess that it was him. A lord did not dress like that, surely?

The man walking to her was not wearing a hat, and had mud splattered across his face. He was wearing breeches and a greatcoat that looked as though they had been out of fashion when his father had been a young man, and they were patched and frayed so many times that it was difficult to see just how much of the original coat was left.

There was a glower on his face that was most unbecoming, but it disappeared into discomfort when their eyes met.

Arabella gasped. Well, even under all those old clothes and the mud, Lord Nathaniel Cartier was very handsome. A sharp jawline and a serious mouth were accompanied by eyes that glittered with intelligence, and the entire effect was…mesmerizing.

Something uncomfortable stirred in her stomach. A little unorthodox, perhaps, Arabella told herself, but then he was at home, in his own surroundings. Perhaps he had forgotten that she was to arrive today.

There was no knowing what old sort of gown she might throw on in a morning if she did not believe she was to see anyone interesting.

"Miss Fitzroy, may I introduce you to my son, Lord Nathaniel," said Lord Cartier with a beaming smile. "Son, this is Miss Arabella Fitzroy."

Arabella dropped into a low curtsey—far lower than she was accustomed to, but it felt appropriate. He was a lord, after all, and she a mere miss.

Besides, he was her future husband.

Her future husband. Arabella shivered slightly as she straightened up from her curtsey.

"Oh, my dear, you must be freezing—let us get you inside," said Lady Cartier suddenly, stepping forward to put an arm around her and usher her toward the front door. "Come on, Nathaniel."

The four of them went up the steps and into the hall of Oxcaster Lacey, which was quite large enough to fit Arabella's entire home. She swallowed. This was going to take some getting accustomed to. What if she could not find her way to her room? Even worse, what if she could not find her way to the breakfast room in the morning?

"I really must go and finish some letters," Lady Cartier was saying.

Arabella blinked. Without her noticing, Lord Cartier had entirely disappeared, and his wife was drifting toward a door which led to a room which could have been a drawing room.

"I am sure my son will be able to acquaint you with your surroundings and show you to your suite," said Lady Cartier before shutting the door and leaving the two of them alone.

Arabella swallowed, then smiled at Lord Nathaniel. He was standing right by the front door, hardly having taken a step inside. The glower had returned.

"Well," Arabella said aloud, inviting him to say something. Anything.

But Nathaniel stayed silent. There was an awkwardness in his bearing, now she came to look at him more closely, that clearly showed his lack of comfort with the whole situation. He did not need to say that he wished she were not here, Arabella thought with a flush to her cheeks.

His demeanor made that quite obvious.

"Well," she repeated, shrugging off her pelisse because it appeared he was not going to offer to assist her. "Is there a place I can put this, or…"

More silence. Arabella did not believe she was asking a particularly difficult question, and though she felt the awkwardness of the situation herself, she was at least able to speak.

Nathaniel was just standing there like…like a lemon. As though he had no idea she had been coming at all and was now utterly at a loss for words at her appearance.

Arabella tried to smile. A little light conversation, that was all they needed. It was a rather strange experience, after all, meeting one's future spouse in such circumstances. There were not that many marriages arranged these days, at least not in her circles.

All they had to do was talk to each other. She was certain, after a few minutes, she would quickly see the charms of the man whose very look was making her warm.

"I will just put this here," she said quietly to herself, placing the pelisse on a chair by the door. "Now, Nathaniel—I mean, Lord Nathaniel—"

"Nathaniel is sufficient."

If Arabella had not been watching closely and seen the man's mouth move, she would not have been entirely sure that he had spoken. His syllables were so clipped, his sentence so brief, it was hard to believe that he was the son of such an elegant woman.

"Nathaniel," said Arabella, trying to slow her heartbeat. It was not her responsibility to make this go well, at least not entirely. He had to bear some of the weight of the conversation.

Did he not?

"Thank you for meeting me as I arrived," she said softly.

"I didn't," said Nathaniel curtly. "To be quite honest, Miss Fitzroy, I had entirely forgotten you were coming."

"Oh," said Arabella helplessly.

Well, where did she go from here? She was not her sister Caroline, able to speak to absolutely anyone on any subject, always able to make them feel at ease. Nor was she Lucy, whose mischievous nature could usually get people to laugh and break the tension of a room.

If only she could think of what to say—but it was all too overwhelming. Oxcaster Lacey, Lord and Lady Cartier, the woodland, the lakes—and now this man.

Nathaniel pulled off his greatcoat to reveal what appeared to be a farmer's smock, just as dirty as his face, and a large leather belt around his breeches which had seen better days.

But none of that would have been so interesting if Arabella had not been so transfixed by the man himself.

If Lord Nathaniel Cartier had been wearing the typical clothes of a man of his station—shirt, waistcoat, jacket, cravat—then she would have been able to see a little of his figure, and not much more.

But he was not, and as such, Arabella had a far more intimate view of the man standing before her.

It was not purely mud, therefore, but a dark scratchy beard that coated his face, descending down his neck and into his smock. Arabella swallowed. She had never seen a gentleman's neck like that, utterly unadorned, no cravat protecting his dignity.

And speaking of protecting his dignity, the smock was loose fitting, but the sleeves were rolled up, revealing strong forearms with a sprinkling of dark hair. Nathaniel's hands were large, strong. She could see a few calluses on them, as though he had been working as hard as his smock suggested.

All in all, the very picture of manhood.

Arabella swallowed. Was it just her, or was it getting warm, even without her pelisse?

What would it be to be held in those arms—touched by those hands—kissed by a mouth surrounded by beard?

Heat flushed through her, and Arabella was certain that her cheeks had pinked, but she could not help it. It was natural, wasn't it, to wonder about these things?

They were engaged to be married, after all. He must have thought about it. They would not merely be sharing a life together, but a bed. They would make love, make children. They would know each other far more intimately than anyone else in the world.

And if she was to do such things, would she enjoy them? Would he please her, pleasure her, make her feel—

"Miss Fitzroy?"

Arabella started. Nathaniel had taken an awkward step toward her, concern on his face. Evidently, she had been thinking too long.

She cleared her throat. "I am a little tired from the journey."

Nathaniel nodded. "You should rest. Dinner will be at seven."

Arabella smiled. Dinner at seven. She was not certain she would be able to sit before such a fine specimen of a man and have a reasonable conversation. Not when she had so many questions. Questions only he could answer.

"And after dinner, I hope we will have the chance to talk together. Just the two of us, I mean," Arabella said with what she hoped was a winning smile. "There are so many things I wish to ask, to know about you—though I suppose as I am staying for Christmas, we will have plenty of time."

Nathaniel took another few steps toward her, until he stood right before her. Arabella's breath caught in her throat. He smelled of the countryside and hard work and a job well done. He smelled…of woodsmoke and barley and something else she could not make out.

"Really?" he said coldly. "And just what do we have to discuss?"

Was he teasing? That was always the trouble, Arabella thought, with meeting a new person. One never knew quite what their sense of humor was.

"Why, our engagement, of course," Arabella said with a wry smile. "I was always told that correspondence was out of the question before we met in person, a rule my father put into place, do not ask me why, but that has meant that naturally I have many questions."

Nathaniel looked down at her imperiously, and Arabella swallowed. What it would be like to be kissed by those lips, rough and sweet at the same time. She shivered.

"Ah yes, the engagement," said Nathaniel in a low voice. Arabella could not help but watch his lips as he spoke. "If it goes ahead. If I like what I see, of course. Dinner at seven, Miss Fitzroy."

He strode away from her before Arabella could reach out and grab him—something she certainly would have done to make him stay and talk to her like a reasonable gentleman.

"If you like—excuse me, Lord Nathaniel, if you like what you see?" Arabella called after him as Nathaniel strode across the hall to the stairs. "What on earth do you mean by that?"

He turned at the base of the stairs, and she was struck by just how handsome he was—a distracting thought that she tried to push aside. A gentleman could not be handsome if he was so rude and infuriating as this man. Could barely be a gentleman!

"I am under no illusion of the agreement our parents made, Miss Fitzroy, but an agreement can be unmade," Nathaniel said curtly. "It was not of my doing. It could be my undoing. I will not be at dinner, good night."

Arabella stared, unable to speak and utterly incensed, as her supposed future husband walked away from her. The cheek of it! The very outrage that he may look at her and find her wanting— when she was at least dressed like a lady and had been warm and polite.

Narrowing her eyes, Arabella sighed heavily. She would prove herself to this man and had the entirety of Christmas to do it.

CHAPTER THREE

ARABELLA STARED AT the looking glass. It was framed in gold gilt, with little cherubs at the top, painted gold, who were playing trumpets.

To announce her beauty, she thought wryly, tugging at one sleeve of her gown that did not seem to want to match the other. It was most irritating. One of the few times in her life she actually cared what she looked like, when there was someone there to look good *for*, and nothing seemed to be working.

Arabella sighed and dropped onto the red velvet-covered stool that sat before the large mirror. Lady Cartier had been kindness itself, of course.

"And I'll send my lady's maid," she had said after rescuing Arabella, finding her wandering in a corridor because Nathaniel had not shown her to her suite. "She will be able to get you ready for dinner tonight."

Which was all very well, thought Arabella, but evidently her ladyship required a great deal of getting ready, for it was a quarter to seven now, and the lady's maid had not appeared.

She had done the best she could on her own. It was not like the Fitzroys had enough lady's maids for each of their daughters. Even with Jemima and Caroline married, there were only two for the four remaining sisters, and Arabella had become quite accustomed to sharing with little Sophia.

But still. There was only so much one could do to the back of one's hair without a second person holding a mirror, Arabella thought ruefully as she attempted to turn her head from one side to the other to see what mess she had made.

Throwing down a pin onto the toilette table, Arabella gave it up as a bad job. Well, it was not as though Nathaniel—Lord Nathaniel—was going to be staring at the back of her head all dinner.

Arabella sat up a little straighter. No, he would be looking at her. Forced to look at her and talk to her. Perhaps then she would be able to charm him a little. Get him to talk, at least. If he attended at all. She was still not certain whether he had been jesting when he had said he would not come to dinner.

She smiled to herself, a little wistfully. It was her bad luck that the man to whom she was engaged was an absolute delight to look at himself.

If only his powers of conversation were equal to his looks.

"Ah yes, the engagement. If it goes ahead. If I like what I see, of course. Dinner at seven, Miss Fitzroy."

Arabella cleared her throat and looked away from her reflection, turning on the stool to look around her suite. There was only so long one could stare at one's own face, after all. Especially when it became obvious she was blushing.

Half in an attempt to remove her thoughts from the irritatingly handsome man she had met downstairs, Arabella looked about the suite. Her jaw had dropped the first moment she had arrived, the double doors pushed open to show it off at its best.

Lady Cartier had not been exaggerating when she had called it a suite. The bedchamber itself was large and opened up into a little sitting room that was most pleasant, with a westerly aspect that would be gorgeous in the early winter afternoons.

Everything was luxurious; there was evidently money in the Cartier family. They had even put paper and sealing wax, along with two pens and ink, on the desk that sat in the corner. Mahogany. Nothing but the best.

"So, you can write to your family over Christmas," Lady Cartier had said with a bright smile. "I certainly would wish to write to my husband and son if I were apart from them at this time of year. See you at dinner!"

And so, she had departed, probably not realizing the pain she had caused in Arabella's heart.

Her heart twisted again now. She did feel very alone in this large suite all by herself. Her family were near on a hundred miles away, most of them at Chalcroft, the others at Caroline's side.

She was probably an aunt now, she realized with a lurch. Caroline had undoubtedly had her baby, if everything had gone well, and that would make her an aunt. When would they write and tell her all? Did she have a niece or nephew?

"Oh, miss, I am ever so sorry!"

Arabella turned, startled, to stare at the slightly disheveled lady's maid who had careered into the door, almost taking it off its hinges by the look of things.

"I completely forget how the mistress asked me a to come to you after I had finished with her, and I was just having my dinner and the housekeeper asked me what you were like, and I realized I clean forgot!" said the lady's maid in a hurried rush. "Quick, we only have five—who did that to your hair?"

Arabella, realizing whatever she had done to her hair was now visible in the looking glass behind her, flushed. "I tried to—"

"We can fix it," said the lady's maid firmly, seeming to get a grip on herself. "Turn around now, there's a lamb."

And so, within seven minutes—Arabella could not begrudge the lady's maid the additional time, she had managed to remove far more pins lodged in her hair than she ever remembered putting in there—she was ready for company.

"There," said the lady's maid with a flourish. "I can do no better."

Which was not precisely a resounding sign of approval, but Arabella had to take it. She had no other choice. The dinner gong had been rung a few minutes ago, and she had absolutely no idea how long it would take her to get down to the dining room.

"Here we go," she muttered under her breath as she stepped into the corridor and turned right. "Time to face—"

"Left!" came a helpful voice from her suite. "Along, down the steps, left, second right, and straight on, and you'll see the door ahead!"

Arabella did her best to remember these instructions, but her mind was swirling with so many questions about the strange and unknown Lord Nathaniel that she managed to misremember the instructions. It was only when a kindly footman happened upon her, utterly lost in the library, did she eventually make it to the door of the dining room.

She was hot. She felt rather uncomfortable in the most fashionable of gowns that she had been able to borrow from Caroline. She knew she was late.

It was not an auspicious beginning, but Arabella was determined to improve things. After all, how could they be much worse?

Opening the door, Arabella smiled at Lord and Lady Cartier who were already seated. "I hope I am not too late."

Lord Cartier rose to his feet as she entered, but there was a frown on his face that she did not understand until he asked, "But where is Nathaniel?"

Arabella halted her footsteps. Was she supposed to know? Was she his keeper already, this gentleman who did not appear to wish to be her husband at all, even before they had exchanged vows in a church?

"Nathaniel," his mother repeated as though Arabella had momentarily forgotten him.

"Yes, Lord Nathaniel," Arabella said, unsure whether she was supposed to sit down or remain standing where she was. "What about him?"

"Well, he was supposed to meet you outside your suite and escort you downstairs," said Lady Cartier with a slightly nervous smile. "Did he…did he not meet you?"

Arabella forced a smile. He was a rude, irritating, thoughtless gentleman, and she saw absolutely no reason why she should go through with this foolish betrothal if he was going to be so insolent!

"I am afraid he did not," she said sweetly. "It appears we missed each other."

"Nothing of the sort," said a deep voice behind her. "I did not meet you. Good evening, Father."

Arabella turned in a swish of skirts and saw the ironic smile on Lord Nathaniel Cartier's face. He could not have presented a more different picture than the first time she had seen him but mere hours ago.

Where the dirt had been, there was now only a sardonic look on his face, the beard still intact—but the delicious way it disappeared down his neck and onto his chest was hidden by a cravat tied in a most complex knot.

The waistcoat and jacket he had chosen—or, Arabella reminded herself, his valet had likely chosen—were a delicate light blue, perfectly suiting his eyes. His shirt was clean, and a shirt, not a smock. The mud-dripping boots were gone, and he was…he was perfect.

Blast, thought Arabella, her heart skipping a beat most painfully. He was perfect. *Damn.*

"I thought you said you were not coming to dinner," she hissed under her breath, heart racing.

Why did he manage to have this sort of effect on her? It was most unfair that the man she was supposed to marry was both rude and handsome.

"I thought you said we must have missed each other," he quipped with a lazy grin as he stepped around her toward the dining table. "Mother."

"Nathaniel, you are both late and rude," said Lady Cartier with a frown that Arabella could see had very little heart in it.

Her son shrugged as he sat between his parents, leaving the seat opposite him empty. "That I am."

Arabella took a long, deep, calming breath. This was not as bad as it looked, though it might be as bad as it felt. The fact was, Lord Nathaniel Cartier had taken against her for some reason. That much was obvious. Why exactly, she could not tell—but perhaps he was even less enthusiastic than she was about this arrangement.

It was not unsurprising. Arranged marriages were becoming less common now, no matter what Miss Theodosia Ashbrooke said.

Still, this was the situation they found themselves in, and Arabella was not going to let her father down. He had made it very clear this match had been made long ago with the agreement of all parents, and so it was now time for her to carry it out.

Even in the face of such…such…

"Miss Fitzroy?"

Arabella started. Evidently, Lady Cartier had been speaking to her, but she had been completely lost in her own thoughts. "I beg your pardon?"

"I said, do sit down, dear," said Lady Cartier.

"Sit down," repeated Arabella. She heard Nathaniel snort, and tried desperately to pull herself together. She was not the foolish one in this arrangement! "Yes, of course. Thank you."

She tried to move across the room as elegantly as she could manage, which was no easy feat when her legs felt weak. What had she managed to get herself into?

For a brief moment as Arabella sat down at the highly decorated table with more forks on the left of her plate than she had ever seen together, she thought wistfully of Chalcroft.

Her family was there, the whole family. Almost every Fitzroy: laughing, joking, teasing Esther something dreadful about those novels she liked to read, or Olivia for how she simply must have the best of everything.

And here she was. At a table more richly dressed, about to eat food in more complicated recipes, while drinking wine of surely a superior vintage…

Arabella sighed, whilst forcing a smile on her face. She knew where she would rather be.

That was the strange thing about other people's dinners. They were always so different from what one was accustomed to. Growing up with five sisters, Arabella was accustomed to a dining table full of conversation, usually at least two happening together, with much back and forth, debate, argument, laughter.

So, when the soup arrived and the Cartiers began eating in absolute silence, Arabella thought for a moment they had paused to pray.

But no, they were eating their soup, elegantly of course, with their little fingers sticking out each time they lifted a spoon to their mouths…but they made not a sound.

Arabella tried the soup. It was very good, but it did not make up for the complete lack of conversation.

"What delicious soup," Arabella said with a bright smile. "You will have to permit me to ask your cook for the recipe to take back for our housekeeper."

Lady Cartier gave her a smile in response, but said nothing, dropping her gaze to her bowl of soup.

Arabella swallowed. Surely this was not normal! But then, she had little experience of dining out other than with London families, all much like the Fitzroys. Was this what the nobility did? Eat their meals in complete silence, ignoring all opportunities to converse and get to know each other?

For she did wish to know them. Why, this would be her family in a few short months. Her Papa had not been direct about when the wedding would take place, but her Mama had mentioned a June wedding.

June. That meant six months before she would come to live here.

Arabella's stomach gave a lurch that had nothing to do with the soup. *Here.* This would be her home; she would learn to love its corridors, she was sure, and the different views from the large windows. She would learn the paths through the woodland, perhaps recognize the deer by their antlers, name all the swans.

But could she be happy? Could anyone be truly happy in the face of such…such silence?

"And what has occupied you today, Lord Nathaniel?" she asked politely.

She did not, however, receive a polite response. In fact, she did not receive any. Despite Arabella looking kindly, and then pointedly at the man opposite her, Nathaniel did nothing but eat his soup.

Well, perhaps she was expecting too much of them, Arabella tried to think charitably, as a knot of tension starting tightening in her stomach. She was a stranger, after all, and not everyone was chatty the moment that they met new people.

Perhaps it would all be different when the main course came out.

But after the footmen gently deposited what looked like grouse on their plates and started serving the family vegetables, Arabella found almost every attempt she made buffeted back to her.

"And are the grounds extensive, Lord Nathaniel?" she asked finally, thinking she would be in dire straits if she was forced to resort to discussing the weather.

Nathaniel glanced at her, his light blue eyes almost crystal as they gazed at her. He appeared to be trying to decide whether or not she was worthy of a response, but after a glare from his mother, he said curtly, "Yes."

Arabella waited for more, but once again, that appeared to be all he was willing to share. "Yes?"

He nodded. "Yes."

And that was that. It was so infuriating, Arabella considered rising to her feet and announcing to the entire room, footmen and all, that this entire engagement nonsense was clearly a mistake, and she would be more than happy to call the whole thing off, as he was so clearly not interested in pursuing it.

Just as she opened her mouth, Arabella caught his gaze.

She closed her mouth. There was something there, something deep. Something far more interesting than anything Nathaniel had said, that was for sure.

He looked at her with a longing, a desperation, a heat that made Arabella's cheeks pink and her heart flutter in her chest. He looked at her as though she was the only woman in the world, the only person in the world.

As though he had been waiting for her all these years and was desperate to be alone with her, at once, so that he could tell her—tell her what?

A secret flittered across his face and then it was gone before Arabella could even guess what it was.

Nathaniel looked away.

Arabella found her breath caught in her throat, and she tried to force herself to breathe naturally as she finished her last mouthful of this course with a fork she had never seen before.

What had that been about? How was it possible for a gentleman to be so sullen and silent, yet at the same time, so open and vulnerable?

"Do make some conversation, boy," said Lord Cartier, evidently forgetting he had contributed absolutely nothing to the table. "Say something, and something the rest of us will actually want to hear, not any of your nonsense."

Nathaniel flushed, the skin under his beard darkening, and Arabella leaned forward, intrigued.

His nonsense? So, there were topics that Lord Nathaniel happily spoke on—but not ones that his parents approved of. Interesting. What on earth could that be? Was that why her betrothed was so silent? Because he had been told not to speak on certain things before her?

What was Lord Nathaniel Cartier hiding?

"I would be very interested to hear a little nonsense," Arabella said warmly, trying to laugh as naturally as possible. "I would be interested in anything you had to say, Nathaniel."

Their eyes met once more, and this time Arabella was certain.

He was attracted to her; at least, he thought her pretty.

Yet he said nothing. Nathaniel's gaze dropped to his plate and he stayed silent.

Lady Cartier cleared her throat. "What wonderful weather we are having, Miss Fitzroy, for the time of year."

And there we go, Arabella thought sadly as she smiled weakly. The weather. They had reached the very bottom of the barrel and there was nowhere else to go from here. She would need to find something—anything—to talk about.

"What do you think of Christmas weddings, Nathaniel?"

Lord and Lady Cartier both dropped the cutlery they were holding, but Arabella paid them no heed. She was too busy watching their son.

Nathaniel slowly placed down his knife and fork and looked at her. There was a wry, almost rueful look on his face, as though he had warned her not to speak on this topic, and she had chosen to ignore him.

But that was not the case. The man had barely spoken to her enough for her to have any idea what his opinions were on topics of conversation.

And it was time that changed, Arabella thought to herself. Time to ignore the rules.

"I think matrimony itself, much like Christmas, is something to be respected," Nathaniel said slowly in his deep voice as his parents exchanged worried glances. Arabella could see them out of the corner of her eye, but she was far more interested in him. "And I believe that they should be separate."

"Interesting," said Arabella brightly. "So, you would prefer a summer wedding?"

"I would prefer no wedding at all," said Nathaniel darkly.

Before she could say any more, he pushed back his chair, threw down his napkin, and strode to the door.

"Nathaniel!" Arabella could not help it; though it was far beyond the etiquette and decorum which she had been taught, it was most grievously upsetting to find the man who she had been told would be marrying her so clearly not interested in matrimony at all.

What was the point in her father sending her here, if only to be humiliated?

Nathaniel halted at the door, his hand on the handle, and took a deep breath. Without turning around, he said in his deep voice, "I apologize, Miss Fitzroy, but I believe you have been brought here under false pretenses. As I said when you arrived, any agreement that has been made can be unmade."

"So, is that what you are doing?" asked Arabella fiercely, rising to her feet, trying to keep her temper down but feeling it rise within her chest, hot and sticky and ready to blast from her lips. "Is this you ending this agreement?"

"No," said Nathaniel heavily. "Not yet."

"This is what you meant when you said you were going to see what you liked?" Arabella said, ignoring the astonished cries of Lord and Lady Cartier. "Did it ever occur to you, my lord, that I may be the one who does not like what I see?"

Nathaniel did turn at that, and Arabella found to her own disgust that she very much liked what she saw.

"It did not occur to me," said Nathaniel lightly. "Something interesting for me to consider. Good night."

CHAPTER FOUR

ARABELLA MANAGED TO find her way back to her suite. Someone had turned down the bed, placed a bed warming pan in it, and gone through her trunk to find her nightgown and laid it out on the sheets.

She would put up with Lord Nathaniel Cartier for as long as she could, and then she would write to her father and ask—and demand that she return home immediately.

Or even better, go straight to Chalcroft. Surely it would not take long for a carriage to get her there, and then she could pretend this entire thing never happened.

As Arabella's eyes closed, a face appeared in her mind. A haughty face, with a dark beard and light eyes.

Arabella's eyes snapped open, but in the darkness of her bedchamber the vision of Nathaniel's face kept appearing, no matter what she tried to force him out.

"I apologize, Miss Fitzroy, but I believe you have been brought here under false pretenses. As I said when you arrived, any agreement that has been made can be unmade."

It was in the early hours of the morning, therefore, that Arabella was able to fall asleep, and when she awoke it was in a very bad temper, with red eyes and heavy bags beneath them.

"Oh, blow," Arabella muttered as she caught sight of herself in the rather large looking glass by the toilette table.

She looked…well, awful. She was certain her sister Jemima would have had a few choice words to describe just how terrible she looked, but thankfully, Arabella was alone, and could merely imagine the descriptors.

That was the trouble with having red hair, she thought ruefully. When one also had red eyes, the whole effect was rather…unfortunate.

But still, she had no choice but to bathe her eyes and dress herself in her most formal cotton gown. She may have to send back to London for more gowns at this rate, Arabella thought as she finished buttoning herself up, thanking her lucky stars this gown was buttoned at the side, as the lady's maid had not made another appearance. She could not be expected to stay in a place as luxurious and stately as Oxcaster Lacey without a wider collection of gowns.

Breakfast was a quiet affair. Arabella had already learned that mealtimes with the Cartiers were to be taken, in the main, in silence, and though it took her three attempts to find the breakfast room—finally pointed in the right direction by a kindly maid—Arabella did not look up from her plate during the meal.

Nathaniel did not attend.

It was on the tip of her tongue to ask Lord and Lady Cartier precisely where they thought their son was, and why they believed it acceptable for him to talk to her as he had last night.

His words rang in Arabella's ears, and her cheeks pinked as she sipped her tea and recalled her own.

"Did it ever occur to you, my lord, that I may be the one who does not like what I see?"

"It did not occur to me. Something interesting for me to consider. Good night."

It was outrageous, Arabella thought viciously as she stabbed at a roasted tomato—a real luxury in December, she had no idea how they had managed it.

After all, she was the one who had come all this way to meet him—to meet them, she corrected herself silently. She was the one who had sacrificed a family Christmas, and a Christmas at Chalcroft no less.

And she was the one who was being examined, being judged?

Arabella was furious, which was why she was not currently admitting to herself that Lord Nathaniel Cartier was probably well within his right to do so.

It did not take an intelligent person to see from the state of Oxcaster Lacey—nor the fact that he had a title—that Nathaniel was her social superior. The thought burned in Arabella's mind, irritating her but making it impossible for her to ignore.

Her sister may be a countess, but that had been a surprise to everyone—and the Fitzroys were now considered by most of the *ton* to have married her beyond her class.

He was the one who would be marrying lower than his status, Arabella reminded herself, no matter how much she hated the thought. Of course, he wished to review her, like a painting he would consider purchasing.

She would need to be suitable. Was that perhaps why her father had not wished to send one of her sisters with her?

The thought made Arabella's stomach drop most painfully. Did her Papa know that this was the tack Nathaniel would take, and was concerned, perhaps, that the distraction of one of Arabella's more beautiful sisters would complicate matters?

Arabella stabbed at a sausage, a grim look on her face.

"Goodness, what did that sausage ever do to you?" remarked Lord Cartier with what he obviously thought was a genial smile.

"Where is your son?" Arabella said in reply.

The moment she had spoken, she knew she had spoken too rudely, too abruptly.

Lord Cartier's face went pale, and he instantly looked at his wife.

"Ah," said Lady Cartier, dabbing at her mouth with her napkin.

Why do they not want me to know where Nathaniel is? And then the answer came to her; it was so obvious, she wondered why she had not considered it before. Wasn't it clear?

Lord Nathaniel had a mistress. It was the only answer. No wonder he was always late to be here, why he avoided her presence, why he did not wish to consider the possibility of matrimony.

Perhaps he wished to wed this young lady, Arabella thought wildly as Lady Cartier murmured something about being very busy.

Yes, busy, Arabella thought with a wry smile. That is one word for it.

For some strange reason, the realization that Nathaniel was in love with another slightly calmed Arabella's pained heart. Yes, it was a slight snag in the plans for their betrothal and eventual marriage, but at least it was not personal. Not personal to her, at any rate.

Why, any Fitzroy sister could have arrived, even Lucy who was considered by many to be the prettiest, and Nathaniel would have been equally unimpressed with her appearance.

The thought gave Arabella hope. He could not marry this woman, whoever she was, of that she was certain. If Lord and Lady Cartier approved of the harlot, they would have announced that engagement already, written to her father to break off their agreement.

So, they did not approve of the mistress. And that meant, in time, Nathaniel could learn to approve of her.

"—somewhere about here," Lady Cartier said vaguely, waving an arm about. "You know, I must say how pleased I am that our families will be united."

"Yes, yes, very pleased," said Lord Cartier hastily, jumping onto the topic eagerly.

Arabella looked between them. She was not sure how the two older people could possibly believe, at this moment, that the marriage was going ahead. Had they not heard their own son speak so disparagingly of the match only yesterday?

"You do me great honor," she said awkwardly, hardly knowing what to say.

"Yes, it was planned so long ago, and now the time is finally here," said Lady Cartier with a smile. "At least, almost here. I agree with your mother, June is such a wonderful time for a wedding."

"Though if we need to make it…I don't know, an autumn wedding," said Lord Cartier with some unease and a meaningful look at his wife.

Arabella looked between the two of them. Why could they not just say it? Why could they not admit to her that the meeting between herself and Nathaniel had certainly not gone to plan, and now the entire wedding was up in the air?

"Well, we shall have to see what Lord Nathaniel thinks," Arabella said brightly. She would not let them see how upset last night's dinner had made her. She would not permit anyone to see how alone she felt in this large, rambling house. "I suppose I will see him this morning?"

Lady Cartier hesitated just a little too long before saying slowly, "I am sure if you just meandered the grounds, or the house…"

And so that is what she did. Arabella spent the next two days meandering through the grounds, looking—not precisely hunting, but looking—for her betrothed.

The woodland scenery was beautiful. Wintery light fell softly through the bare branches, and a few times, Arabella spotted deer grazing just ahead. She would halt, watching her breath billow up before her in the cold winter air, and gaze at the elegant animals until a twig cracked, or a bird flew past singing its warning call, and they would be gone.

The house was beautiful. Oxcaster Lacey, one of the maids told her, had been built during Queen Elizabeth's reign and had been left almost intact since then. There were many beautiful rooms, a Long Gallery with the most splendid portraits, and even a library that occupied a whole corner of the house, huge windows pouring onto the many books.

But it was the lake that drew Arabella most often. In the hours that she was left alone, wandering around in an attempt to find a gentleman who was so clearly avoiding her, the lake offered a sense of peace that she was missing.

On the third day of her visit, Arabella stood by the lakeside, the swans swimming elegantly just before her, all seven of them. She was starting to get to know them now, so many hours of hers had been spent here.

"Hello," she whispered, more to have the excuse to speak aloud than anything else. Conversation was in short supply at Oxcaster Lacey.

Arabella sighed. It was not that she was upset by the idea that Nathaniel had a mistress, not exactly.

So many gentlemen had mistresses; it had almost become the fashionable thing to do in London. Arabella had overheard Lady Romeril once say that Mr. Fitzroy, her father, was most unfashionable by refusing to take one, which had made her smile.

But it was certainly not unheard of, and Arabella was old enough to know that one's affection for a mistress, particularly before one had married, said nothing about the affection of one's wife.

At least, that was what she kept telling herself. Why there was a twist in her stomach every time the word "mistress" echoed in her mind, or why her heart contracted painfully whenever she thought that Nathaniel had shared with another that exquisite pleasure she had thought promised to her…she could not say.

Arabella swallowed and tried to forget the knot in her stomach as she watched the beautiful birds swim by her.

She was not upset.

She was lonely. Living in a…well, her father would call it a "compact" house with six sisters and then, after two marriages, four sisters meant Arabella was far more accustomed to noise, shrieks, laughter, arguments, and general busyness than she had ever realized.

Now she was here, in a large manor house in which she could shout at one end and no one would hear her, which was rather alarming.

Arabella had not written to them yet. She would as soon there was something worth writing about. But the last thing she wanted was to admit to all those at Chalcroft enjoying Christmas that she was miserable.

"You would never have to endure an arranged marriage," Arabella murmured to the swans, in no expectation of a reply. "You can simply do whatever you want."

"Swans mate for life, you know."

Arabella froze. She had thought herself entirely alone, or she would not have spoken aloud. But even though she had only heard the possessor of that voice speak a handful of times, the exact timbre was seared into her mind. Into her heart.

Stomach twisting most painfully, Arabella turned to see Lord Nathaniel standing behind her.

He was dressed once again in the ridiculously strange outfit he had been wearing when she had first met him, though this time the greatcoat was unbuttoned, giving Arabella immediate visibility of his throat, that tantalizing hair disappearing down his smock.

Arabella swallowed. She was not going to permit herself to be attracted to Nathaniel Cartier. He did not deserve that. He did not deserve her.

Such a shame he was so handsome.

"I beg your pardon?" she said stiffly.

"Swans," said Nathaniel, pointing unnecessarily at the large white birds. "They mate for life."

Arabella could not help it; at the word "mate," her cheeks flooded with heat and presumably, color.

Well, really! It was not seemly for a gentleman to say such a word to a lady, let alone a lady alone with him, a lady who was engaged to be married to said gentleman!

It made all sorts of ideas rush through her mind, ideas that

Arabella knew she certainly shouldn't be thinking about. About touching his cheek and feeling the roughness of his beard. About kissing that cheek, his lips, tasting him. Feeling his hand on her waist, pulling her closer. Removing that smock slowly—

"Miss Fitzroy?"

Arabella started and flushed even darker as she saw Nathaniel's curious expression. Well, it was his fault to begin with!

"I did not know that," she said coldly. "About swans."

"Oh, yes, they are fascinating creatures," said Nathaniel curtly as he stepped toward the lake shore to stand beside her.

Arabella shivered, but Nathaniel made no movement to touch her or even acknowledge her presence. He merely stood there, looking out at the lake. Watching the swans swimming.

She cleared her throat, inviting him to say something more, but silence continued.

Eventually, she took matters into her own hands. Well, if they were to be married, and that felt less and less likely with every passing moment, they were going to have to get accustomed to each other.

He would have to accept that she was talkative, that was all.

"M-Mating…mating for life," Arabella said, her tongue slipping over the first word. "Not too dissimilar to humans then, I suppose."

Nathaniel snorted. "Hardly."

She looked up at him. What made a man so prickly and unfriendly as Lord Nathaniel Cartier? Perhaps she had been wrong about the mistress. Perhaps he did wish to marry his harlot, but she had no wish to marry him. Perhaps she had thrown him over when Arabella's visit was announced.

It would certainly explain his animosity to her.

"I suppose there are some people who do not stay faithful," Arabella said pointedly, looking back at the swans. It was easier to watch the graceful birds than look at Nathaniel. "But I like the idea, nonetheless. 'Tis a noble pursuit, the pursuit of true love."

Nathaniel snorted, but said nothing, and Arabella felt her ire only grow. Well, she was doing her best! It was not as though any other Cartier could claim to have done as much to continue conversation as she had—and besides, they were betrothed, even if it was a marriage that had been arranged.

She was the one doing everything right, and Nathaniel? Handsome though he was, infuriating though he was, needed to do something. Do better.

"Have I done something to offend you?" Arabella said suddenly, unable to hold herself back. She turned to Nathaniel, staring pointedly up at him. "You have been nothing but rude and insensitive since I arrived here—as your guest, I may add—and you have been avoiding me ever since."

"No, I haven't," said Nathaniel in a low voice.

"Yes, you have," Arabella insisted. "And I tell you straight, Lord Nathaniel, 'tis tiring. You think I am happy to just wait around for you to decide whether or not I am suitable as a bride?"

He laughed darkly at that. "You have somewhere else you would rather be?"

"Yes," Arabella said bluntly.

That surprised him. A look of momentary shock flashed across his face, but Nathaniel was able to readjust his face almost immediately.

A little shame sparked at Arabella's heart, but she could not help it. Well, really! Did he think she had no other family nor friends with whom to spend the Christmas season? Did he think her desperate, perhaps choosing to come here because there was nowhere else to go?

The very idea!

"I think at the very least, I should know on what criteria I am being judged," Arabella said, a little calmer now. "I believe that only fair."

It was with a glare that Nathaniel turned to her, and only then was Arabella aware of just how very close they were standing. Why, there were but a few inches between them.

Yet she could not step back. There was something intoxicating about being this close to him, a man who appeared part gentleman, part laborer.

Nathaniel's light eyes looked down into hers, as a sardonic smile crept over his face. "You do?"

Arabella nodded, struggling for a moment to find the right words. "I…I do."

Why was it that she was so painfully reminded of the wedding vows in that moment? It was almost as though they were promising each other something, despite the tension between them. Though no wedding, Arabella was sure, would have swans as the only witnesses.

"Well then, Miss Arabella Fitzroy, this is what I think," said Nathaniel softly, not looking away from her eyes. "It may surprise you to know that few gentlemen jump for joy at the thought of being handed a bride as though one had ordered a pipe. I had hopes…have hopes of meeting a woman who is bright and intelligent and beautiful. Who understands nature as I do, who believes as I do that…that…"

She watched him swallow, watched him struggle to find the words.

It was perhaps the longest speech that Nathaniel had given since she had arrived, and Arabella was astonished to hear real feeling in his tones.

He was…frustrated. Irritated, as she had been, that this whole arrangement had been planned. If she was not mistaken, Lord Nathaniel Cartier was a romantic.

The thought astonished her, taking Arabella's breath away. She had never met a gentleman who was a romantic. She had always assumed it was only ladies.

But he appeared genuinely injured that his ability to choose his own mate for life, as perhaps Nathaniel would put it, had been taken from him.

Arabella swallowed. "It…this whole situation is perhaps not one that either of us would have chosen."

Nathaniel laughed gently, his gaze dropping to her mouth.

"No. What I think you forget, Miss Fitzroy, is that a marriage is a long time, and in my mind should be a true partnership. A meeting of hearts. A meeting of minds. A meeting of bodies."

A cool breeze whistled past them, and Arabella shivered, but she knew her movement had nothing to do with the weather.

A meeting of bodies. Heat seared through her as Arabella thought for a moment of what it would be like to kiss that man. A man who infuriated her so much, and yet tantalized her in equal measure.

"And bodies," Nathaniel said in a quiet voice, lowering his head slightly so that their lips were mere inches away from each other, "know what they like without the mind interfering. That's nature, Arabella. That's primal. That is something one cannot organize from the cradle. A man's needs are exquisite, and I need...I need to give and receive pleasure openly and sweetly with my wife."

Arabella could not take her eyes off him, the man who was saying such deliciously terrible things, things she wanted to hear more about. Unconsciously, she leaned forward, leaned toward him, sought to close the gap between them.

"Just one kiss," Nathaniel said, dipping his head lower so that his lips brushed across hers without applying any pressure. "That is all one needs to know. Know whether the tension between two people will explode into pleasure."

Arabella could not help it. She moaned slightly and leaned up on her tip toes.

At that exact moment, Nathaniel stepped back. "And so, I hope you can see, Miss Fitzroy," he said in a normal voice, turning to look at the swans, "that I consider this match naught but something written on paper. I would be grateful if you would leave me alone, rather than seek me out as my parents have evidently instructed you. Good day."

He strode away without a second glance, and Arabella stood, all senses heightened, skin tingling, lips desperately crying out for the kiss they had not received.

CHAPTER FIVE

Dear Papa,

Well, I did precisely what you requested, and came to this awful house packed with terrible people who won't talk to me— and Lord Nathaniel! I do not believe I have had the misfortune to meet anyone so irritating. The man is infuriating. I cannot see a possible way for us to have a civil conversation, let alone a happy marriage.

Arabella looked critically at the paper on the desk before her and sighed heavily. Well, that was probably not a letter she could send. She could hardly imagine her Papa being happy to receive such a letter, and in a way, it was a little unfair.

She thought back to the way Nathaniel had teased her yesterday, the way he had been so rude to her, then so enticing, only to step away from her the moment she realized she wished to kiss him with everything within her.

A shiver rustled up Arabella's spine.

She did not want to kiss him, she told herself, as she pulled a shawl around her shoulders a little more tightly. She did not. Nathaniel was not a man worthy of her kisses.

Even if it would have been her first kiss.

Arabella's gaze dropped once more to the letter. She sighed, screwed up the paper, and dropped it into the wastepaper basket beside her.

She would have to at least try to be a little calmer when it came to writing something to her Papa. He would be expecting her letter any day now, especially as they were getting closer to Christmas.

Wishing she had better news to share, Arabella picked up her pen once more, dipped it in the ink, and tried again.

Dear Papa,

Well, I did precisely what you wanted. I came to Oxcaster Lacey just as you said, and I have been very careful to be polite and kind as you and Mama have raised me. I have been sure not to disgrace you with my conduct.

Arabella hesitated. Well, she just about managed to keep her tongue in check. Perhaps not entirely. But she had done better than what she had wanted to do, which was scream at Nathaniel from the rooftop.

Lord and Lady Cartier are very kind and welcoming to me and have been magnificent enough to give me my own suite in Oxcaster Lacey, which I like very much, though it is a little strange to be so far from the rest of the family.

She did not mention the long, empty corridors, the sense that the house was half empty, nor the fact that she had not yet managed to make her way down to breakfast without getting lost. She did not wish to appear a complete fool.

The gardens are pretty enough, although I believe they would be simply splendid in the summertime. I like the lake the best, where I often watch seven swans a swimming, as though they had not a care in the world.

Unlike me, Arabella thought bitterly.

It was no use. She could not continue on with the letter without mentioning just how difficult Nathaniel was; she would be doing her Papa a discredit if she attempted to lie to him. Besides, he would see through any lies immediately. He knew her too well.

But how precisely to do it? There was no kind way to put it, but he was a cad. A cad! No gentleman would speak to her that way.

A clock chimed just behind her. Arabella glanced around and saw it was half past twelve. It would be luncheon soon, and she would be expected to find her way to the dining room. A seemingly impossible feat.

But first, she must finish the letter.

> *I think it only fair to tell you, Papa, that I have been incredibly disappointed in Lord Nathaniel Cartier. His manners have not been what they ought, and he has not made me feel welcome at all.*
>
> *To the contrary, Lord Nathaniel has made it perfectly clear he would prefer our engagement, such as it is, to be broken off.*
>
> *And I must say I agree with him. I know you and Lord Cartier made the match with the best of intentions, but you could not have known just how abominable that man—I will not call him a gentleman—is.*
>
> *So please, Papa. Write soon, and tell me that I am forgiven, and that the whole thing will be called off.*
>
> *And Happy Christmas, from your affectionate daughter,*
> *Arabella F.*

Arabella looked at the letter carefully. She had said nothing specific, which she hoped was fair on Nathaniel, but at the same time she had not hidden her feelings. She could not go through with it. Not now that she knew Nathaniel had no feelings for her whatsoever—and worse, no intention of even trying to like her.

"Just one kiss. That is all one needs to know. Know whether the tension between two people will explode into pleasure."

Heat seared through Arabella's stomach, toward her legs. It was most callous of the man to say such things to her when he knew he was not going to kiss her.

What a blaggard!

It took but a moment for Arabella to carefully fold the pages of her letter, write the address of Chalcroft on the front, and drop some melted sealing wax onto the fold. She left it there on the desk, cooling, as she walked to the window.

Dreary wintery sunlight was pouring down onto the grounds of Oxcaster Lacey. She smiled listlessly as she looked out at them.

In different circumstances, perhaps, she would feel joyful to look out at this view, her future home.

As it was, all she could think of was how far she was from Chalcroft, from her family. How they would all be celebrating the festive season, and here she was, in a cold, dreary house with a family who did not seem to have any desire to like her whatsoever.

Arabella's eyes drifted over to the lake. Perhaps there would be time for her to walk along its banks and see the birds before luncheon.

And then movement caught her eye. Although it was hard to see any great detail from this distance, there was only one person with that sort of figure.

Nathaniel. He was walking along the banks of the lake slowly, his hands in his pockets, from what Arabella could make out.

She glanced at the letter. Would her father agree to her suggestion; would he call off the match?

Her stomach twisted uneasily, and tension pinched the back of her neck. Arabella knew her father well. His oath was his word, and she had never known him to break it. Though he of course cared about her happiness, he also cared about the fact that he had made this arrangement a good many years ago, and he had never broken a vow before.

Arabella swallowed. There was a very real chance, then, that her Papa would disagree with her, that he would insist the match went ahead.

If that was so, it was probably a wise idea to at least become accustomed to Nathaniel and his strange ways. Just in case.

Arabella sighed as she turned back to the window. Though she may not enjoy it, and she was certain that Nathaniel would not appreciate her company, she owed it to herself to try.

If she was going to be trapped in an arranged marriage, she should at least be able to look back and know that she did everything in her power to make it right.

Grabbing her pelisse and a thick woolen scarf, Arabella trotted down the stairs and out of the front door. The cold air hit her lungs most painfully, and she gasped with a wry smile. She should have guessed the wintery sunlight she had seen from her bedchamber window was not the warm beams she had expected.

It took her a few minutes to reach the lake, but Nathaniel was still there. He looked around as she approached, snorted, and turned back to the water. And then it struck her, the thought which had been tickling at the back of her mind since she had first met him.

"Do you know what I think?" Arabella said cheerfully as she reached him.

Nathaniel sighed without looking around. "That you delight in tormenting me?"

"That you are shy," she said promptly.

She was not entirely sure what had made her think of that, but it had struck her the moment she had seen Nathaniel's hunched shoulders and clear desperation not to look at her as she approached him. This was not a man who enjoyed company.

Perhaps she should have worked it out sooner. After all, she had been at Oxcaster Lacey four days, and no one had come to call. There were no neighbors close by; the grounds were too extensive. And besides…

"You are an only child?"

"What of it?" snapped Nathaniel.

Arabella sighed. He truly was going to be an irascible husband if the match went ahead. "Well, I am one of six sisters. I have always had to share, to take turns, been surrounded by noise and laughter and chatter. And tears," she added fairly. "Lots of tears."

There was a strange sort of sound from Nathaniel as a pair of geese sauntered before them on the lake. "What does that matter?"

"Well, I suppose what I mean to say is that I have a great amount of experience with other people," said Arabella quietly. Was this it? Was this the moment that she finally was able to break through that shell of his? "Whereas, I think you have not."

They stood in silence for a few minutes, but this time, Arabella was able to resist the temptation to fill it.

That was always the challenge of being a Fitzroy. There were never silences. Arabella was not entirely sure what to do with them, but she was learning. The best thing to do, at least in the short term, was to keep quiet herself.

Then Nathaniel sighed. "You do not give up, do you?"

"Never," said Arabella cheerfully. "At least, I have not been known to so far, and I do not see why you should be any different."

Her heart leaped slightly as she spoke. Perhaps they would learn to live with each other after all. Perhaps the grouchiness and distrust of her was to be expected. Perhaps the mistress he had been pining over had finally gone.

Then a cloud seemed to cover Nathaniel's face. "Well, I am sorry to disappoint you and ruin your streak of success."

He turned away and started walking along the bank of the lake, away from the house.

Arabella stood for a moment, indecision rushing through her blood. Just how much effort was she willing to put into this man, when she was receiving nothing in return? It was most infuriating.

And yet…there was something about him. Something Arabella could not put into words. Something that made her want…want him.

Heat pooled in her body, a heat she did not understand—or at least, she forced herself not to examine. Because she did not wish to sound like a harlot when she talked about him to her sisters.

And it was that thought, that she would have to explain to her sisters that Lord Nathaniel Cartier had met her and not wished to marry her, that spurred Arabella on.

"Look, the swans," Arabella said, falling into step beside him. "I wonder whether they are all related."

"They are."

Nathaniel had spoken so swiftly, with such energy, that Arabella blinked up at him, certain she had misheard him.

"But…but you probably do not wish to hear about that," he mumbled, looking down.

"No—I do," said Arabella quickly. Any topic, whatever topic, whatever it took to get him to talk to her. "You know their breeding, then?"

"You see those two—that larger one, and that one with the darker bill?" said Nathaniel, halting in his steps and pointing out two of the specific birds.

Arabella looked where he was pointing. "Yes."

"Those are the parents," Nathaniel said warmly. "We only had one swan a few years ago—*cygnus olor*—and after reading more about the species, the genus, their mode of breeding, I decided we needed a female. I wrote to the king—"

"To the king!"

"Yes, all swans are owned by the monarch," said Nathaniel with a grin. "One of those old medieval laws that was created and no one has ever bothered to unmake."

Arabella looked up at him and saw a wry smile on his face.

"I am under no illusion of the agreement our parents made, Miss Fitzroy, but an agreement can be unmade."

She could not help but smile, too. "Well, you would know all about that."

"Securing a breeding pair is difficult, you see, as they mate for life," said Nathaniel enthusiastically, looking away from her and back to the swans. "I could not be sure whether they would bond, you see. One of them had been alone for so long, and the other—"

"Just turned up one day," said Arabella softly.

Well, she could not help it. The story was so perfect, right there—and he was the one who had begun it, after all.

Nathaniel swallowed. She watched his Adam's apple move and shivered slightly at the intensity of the emotion on his face. What was it? Fear? Lust? They seemed so similar in that moment.

"Precisely," he said quietly. "Yet after a few years, we had hatchlings. Three last year, two this summer—at least, two that survived."

Arabella's face fell. "Oh, so there were swanlings which did not survive?"

"Cygnets," corrected Nathaniel. "Not many people know that. Yes, one was got by a fox, and one I think had a disease—I found its body, and after dissecting it—"

"Dissecting it!" Arabella could not help herself—she gasped as she said the word, a little horrified.

Dissected. What sort of gentleman was Lord Nathaniel Cartier, that he could do such a thing?

He looked at her, his gaze hard. "You are offended."

Arabella hesitated. Was she? She was surprised, certainly; it was not every day one had a light conversation with a gentleman about swans which led to a dissection.

But then, she ate beast or fowl every day of her life. She had read...not the entire thing, but a few chapters in books about biology, about the natural world. There was one in the library at Chalcroft. She had seen sketches of rabbit skulls and fox skulls— she had even been to a card party once in a parlor which had a stuffed raven in one corner.

Was what Nathaniel had done any different to those, really?

"No," she said slowly, not looking away from him. "Not offended. Surprised."

Nathaniel let out a bark of a laugh. "Well put, Miss Fitzroy."

"I wish you would call me Arabella."

The words had slipped out before she could stop them— before she had any thought of censoring herself.

But she did. It had been pleasant the other day to have her name on his lips. It gave her a sense of closeness, which she perhaps should have had by now, but had not managed.

There was a wry smile on Nathaniel's lips. "I said before you can call me Nathaniel."

Arabella nodded, suddenly shy. She had never been on a first name terms with a gentleman before. Well, perhaps Orlando, but they did not really count. Friends of the family were not the same as a gentleman one spoke to when one was alone with them.

"So," she said aloud, trying to make sure she did not break the connection, "you are a naturalist, then? A scientific explorer of…of swans?"

"Of all birds, really," said Nathaniel, his features really coming alive as he started to point out different birds on the lake. "And most animals. You see there? Those geese which swam by us a little earlier—they have flown hundreds of miles to be here, to winter here."

Arabella screwed up her nose. "Here? Will they not be cold?"

He laughed at that and shook his head. "They have ventured from far colder climes than we experience—and our swallows, you know, have flown south themselves for warmer climes. Many birds do so."

"But many stay here," Arabella said, hoping to goodness she did not sound a dullard. "The robin, for example. The swans."

Nathaniel nodded. "Yes, and they are perhaps some of our truest birds in England. Robins, *Erithacus rubecula*, and swans will return to the place of their birth to breed the next generation, as do the swallows. The cycle of nature pulling them back, pulling them toward each other."

Arabella swallowed. Only then did she notice how closely they were standing. Why, if she just moved her hand ever so slightly, her fingers would brush against his own.

And she wanted to. In that moment, all she wanted was to fall into his arms, have his fingers entwined in her hair, and feel his lips on hers. Know what it was to be kissed, not just by a man, but by this man. Nathaniel.

For there were hidden depths to him that she was only just beginning to understand. His knowledge was deep, his passion extensive, even if it had taken her a few days to ascertain in which direction it bent. And he was shy. Nervous of her. That was it.

"There are only six swans now."

"What?" Nathaniel asked quickly.

Arabella hesitated. She had spoken only because she had noticed the swans were only six. "Six swans. I thought—you said…seven swans, aren't there?"

He looked at her closely for a moment, then looked back out at the lake. "Yes. There are usually seven swans."

Arabella waited, but he said nothing more. There must be some sort of swan knowledge that made that totally natural. And if Nathaniel could have such interest and passion in birds, could they not meet there? Could she not learn, too, become knowledgeable, perhaps even watch a dissection?

Because, and she knew this to be true as she looked up at him, gazing at the lines creasing at the corners of his eyes as he looked out at the birds on the lake, she could learn to love this man.

Love not purely the handsome expression, the strength in the arms, his ability to make her want him desperately with just a few words. But his intelligence, his wit. The sardonic humor she was sure she would grow to love.

A shiver moved down her neck as Nathaniel turned and smiled, for the first time, without any ruefulness or malice in his eyes. A genuine smile, one directed at her.

"You know, I think this is the longest we have managed to converse without arguing," he said softly.

Arabella smiled weakly. "Are you sure?"

"You're right, perhaps not," he said, his smile becoming mischievous, his light eyes glittering. "There, now you've done it. We're arguing again."

"I think I rather like arguing with you," Arabella admitted.

Nathaniel's smile disappeared, though he did not move away. He looked at her closely, and then finally said, "You know, I think you are trying to seduce me, Arabella."

Arabella shivered. "Perhaps."

She should not have said that word. She should not have been so close to him, should not have been looking at him like that. But she wanted to be.

"And are you prepared?" asked Nathaniel in a low voice, turning to face her, and suddenly putting his hands on her waist. "Are you prepared, Arabella, for what might happen if you do seduce me?"

Arabella could not speak, could not think. All she could do was feel: the searing heat of his hands on her waist, the way he looked at her, a powerful force in itself. And she could feel her desire for him, a desire she had attempted to force down but could no longer fight.

"Yes," she breathed.

It was sudden. Nathaniel dipped his head and crushed his lips on hers, taking her, taking what he wanted, taking passion from her—and Arabella gasped, unable to think, only to taste the desire in him—and the gasp opened her mouth, inviting him in.

Nathaniel needed no further invitation. His tongue slipped into her mouth, teasing her tongue, causing shockwaves of pleasure to rocket through her body.

She clung to him, clung on for dear life. Arabella could almost feel wings sprouting from her back, as they flew on crests of pleasure as the kiss deepened.

And then it was over. Nathaniel released her, stood breathing heavily, staring as though she had bewitched him.

When it was certainly the other way around, Arabella thought wildly, her hand moving to her lips as though to replicate the sense of delicious pressure that he had given her.

"Well, Miss Fitzroy," said Nathaniel in a jagged voice. "You have certainly answered one question for me."

Arabella blinked. Had she asked a question? She could not

recall doing so. "I have?"

A teasing smile lifted a corner of his mouth as Nathaniel offered her his arm. "Did I not tell you that a man could discover all he needed to know about a woman from a kiss? Come. We are late for luncheon. But not a word to my parents about this."

Arabella nodded, hardly able to walk, leaning gratefully on his arm. But one thing rang in her mind; he was still not sure of her. Of this arranged marriage.

If that was not enough for Nathaniel—if a kiss which reached to the very corners of her body, to the tips of her fingers, that made her want to tear her clothes off and offer herself to him—if that kiss was not enough for Nathaniel to know whether he wanted to marry her…

What would be?

CHAPTER SIX

L UNCHEON. SUCH A simple meal.

Arabella sat opposite Nathaniel, trying desperately to remember how to use a knife and fork, as the memory of that kiss haunted her.

"Did I not tell you that a man could discover all he needed to know about a woman from a kiss? Come. We are late for luncheon. But not a word to my parents about this."

"Potatoes?"

Arabella glanced up as she dropped her fork. The heavy clatter on the delicate china made all three Cartiers wince, and she winced herself in sympathetic response.

She really needed to remember that she was seated at luncheon, not on her own and able to daydream. Just because she had been kissed out of her senses by the gentleman sitting opposite her, that wry smile on his face, that did not mean she could completely ignore her surroundings.

Arabella smiled weakly at Lady Cartier. "What delicious potatoes, yes, thank you."

She helped herself rather than waiting for one of the footmen standing at the corners of the room to step forward. She had dined in places with footmen, of course, but it was not the sort of thing she had at home. The Fitzroys were gentry, not nobility.

Arabella placed three more potatoes on her plate to accompany her cold salmon and tried to focus on the simple task of eating. That was all she had to do.

Get through this meal without making a complete and utter fool of herself.

She glanced at Nathaniel, who was grinning most seductively at her across the table.

Arabella dropped her gaze immediately to her food. His parents were right there, on either side of them! What on earth could the man be thinking?

He was a conundrum, he really was. At times taciturn, at other times charming, the only consistent thing about Lord Nathaniel Cartier was that he was completely inconsistent.

A tingle flickered across her heart. If only Arabella did not find that utterly irresistible.

Because he was different, Arabella thought, as she tucked heartily into her salmon and potatoes. She could not say something foolish if her mouth was full of food.

Nathaniel was different from any other man she had ever met, and she had met plenty. One did not live in London in a popular family full of beautiful sisters without receiving a good number of invitations to parties, dinners, luncheons, tea. She even had attended Almack's last Season, which was rather a coup for her mother.

Arabella had not had the heart to tell her that their inclusion was surely due to Caroline's new raised status, as Countess of Cheshire, rather than any individual merit of Arabella's own.

But still. The point was, Arabella thought as she delicately placed a sliver of salmon on her fork, that she had not been entirely ignorant of what gentlemen were like, and she had known precisely the sort of gentleman she had wanted to discover Nathaniel to be.

Kind. Considerate. Caring. A good listener, of course, but also with plenty to say.

And handsome. Attractive. Arabella shivered as she recalled that kiss. A kiss which told her, in no uncertain terms, that she was more than happy to receive his kisses for the rest of her life, if that one was any indication.

Nathaniel certainly knew his way around a woman.

The thought seared through her mind, and Arabella almost dropped her fork again—but the thought this time did not dissipate.

He would know how she wanted to be touched. How she wanted to be kissed. How every inch of her skin could give rise to pleasure, if only he knew how to caress it properly…

"Are you quite well, Miss Fitzroy?"

Arabella started…and dropped her fork.

"You certainly seem most distracted this afternoon," continued Lady Cartier, a look of genuine concern on her face. "You know, what with our plans, I was perfectly happy to leave you to it, but now…"

Nathaniel looked up. "What plans?"

A look passed between Lord and Lady Cartier—a look Arabella did not like. It was the sort of look her parents shared when they had planned something rather unpleasant for their daughters but had not yet told them. Like a visit to an elderly great aunt that no one liked, or an invitation to dine with a family who simply did not have a good cook.

"Well, dear," said Lady Cartier slowly, which only raised the tension in Arabella's shoulders. "You know we have been meaning to visit the Spensers for such a long time—"

"Very old friends of the family," said Lord Cartier in a conspiratorial whisper to Arabella, which carried across the table.

"Very old," said Nathaniel dryly. "I would say they are in their nineties, the pair of them."

"Goodness," said Arabella genuinely. She could not recall ever having met anyone who had reached that old age. "What marvelous specimens."

Heat flooded her cheeks as she realized she had not merely thought but spoken that thought aloud. Nathaniel grinned while Lady Cartier pretended not to have heard.

Well, it was all Nathaniel's fault! Him and his scientific talk only an hour ago, by the lakeside. Was it her fault she could not stop thinking about the way he had spoken with such passion about the natural world?

And kissed her with that same passion?

"Well, we will be going to visit the specimens—the Spensers," corrected Lady Cartier hastily.

Arabella caught Nathaniel's eye, and they shared a look that made her heart flutter. This was a gentleman she could adore, she knew. How utterly frustrating he seemed determined to dislike her, at the very least.

"And as it is such a journey, we will be staying there overnight," Lady Cartier finished.

Arabella looked around suddenly, her mind putting together all the things her hostess had said. If Lord and Lady Cartier were going to visit the Spensers, and they were going to stay overnight, that meant…

She swallowed and tried not to look up at Nathaniel. She knew he would be looking at her, she just knew it. Reviewing her expression. Watching her.

When she did manage to glance up, she immediately looked down again. She knew it.

"I am sure you will not mind entertaining our guest, boy," said Lord Cartier.

Arabella cleared her throat and took a sip of wine, grateful the Cartiers served a bottle with luncheon. She felt in great need of its warming powers now as all heat drained from her.

Lord Nathaniel Cartier and herself, alone, in Oxcaster Lacey…overnight.

It was too much. What did the Cartiers think they were playing at, leaving her alone with a gentleman who oozed sensuality with every passing moment?

Even when he did not want her, he could not help but kiss her. There was something about that man, Arabella thought darkly as she looked at him through her lashes, that made her lose all sense of propriety—not something that was particularly helpful when they were going to spend an unchaperoned evening together.

And an unchaperoned night…

"A chance for the two of you to really get to know each other," said Lady Cartier with a small smile at Arabella, as though she knew how infuriating and confusing her son was being. "Without the two of us getting in the way."

Arabella smiled weakly. Absolutely not. There was no possibility of that happening; she could not let it happen.

What on earth would she do if Nathaniel kissed her like that again? She would surely say something wicked.

"Oh, but it would be such a shame for me to miss the opportunity of making the acquaintance of the Spensers," she said brightly, putting down her wine glass and seeing to her relief that her plate was cleared. No more chances for her to drop her cutlery again. "And Lord Nathaniel can join us, a pleasant trip for the whole—"

"I see no need why I should accompany you all," cut in Nathaniel coldly. "After all, I know the Spensers."

"And we must save some excitement for your next visit, Miss Fitzroy," said Lady Cartier. "After all, we don't want too much excitement in one week."

"But—"

"And the Spensers are only expecting the two of us, and will have prepared a guest chamber for us," interrupted Lord Cartier. "You would not wish for us to impose on the Spensers, I am sure. Especially at their age."

It was on the tip of Arabella's tongue to point out that it would hardly be the Spensers themselves who would be preparing a guest bedchamber—surely, they would have servants for that sort of thing?

"Surely they would have servants for that sort of thing," said Nathaniel lazily, leaning back in his chair.

Arabella blinked. Now that was extraordinary. "Quite," she

said a little breathlessly. "I am sure the four of us—"

"No," said Lady Cartier, firmly. "I am sorry, Miss Fitzroy, but the engagement is one of long standing, and you would not wish for me to change or cancel it, would you?"

Her look was stern, but not in the least as stern as the stares Arabella was daily subjected to by her own mother.

"The engagement is one of long standing, and you would not wish for me to change or cancel it, would you?"

The words rang in her mind, and as Arabella glanced at Nathaniel, she could see that they had made an impression with him as well.

She smiled and saw to her delight that a slight flush tinged his cheeks. Well, that was interesting. It appeared the great and aloof Lord Nathaniel Cartier was not entirely immune to his mother's critiques, nor her charm.

But then her smile fell. Arabella had not cared when she had believed Nathaniel had a mistress and she had only known him as an irritable, detached gentleman. It had not mattered. Her heart had not been touched.

She could still feel the weight and power of his hands on her waist, the way his mouth had taken utter possession of her lips, demanding pleasure from it as well as giving it. His tongue, exquisitely subtle, promising more passion, more pleasure.

Arabella's heart contracted painfully, then returned to its regular rhythm. The idea that Nathaniel would creep off this evening, leaving her alone in this big house, so that he could go and bed his mistress, satisfy his longing and pleasure with her…

It was intolerable.

She felt bound to him, bound in a way Arabella knew they were not. Not yet.

"Well, what fun we will have," said Nathaniel dryly. "Just the two of us and the swans."

Arabella had to smile, and she was rewarded with a brief look of approbation from Nathaniel—but then it was gone.

"Well, I have a little last-minute packing to do," said Lady

Cartier, rising to her feet as her husband and son rose in polite respect.

Arabella almost laughed. Did her ladyship really expect her to believe she packed her own trunk?

"Come on, Cartier," Lady Cartier said briskly. "Off we go, let us leave the young people in peace. Until tomorrow, Miss Fitzroy. Nathaniel—be good."

The two of them had disappeared from the room so quickly that Arabella could not think of anything to say to halt them. It appeared that her long afternoon, evening, and night with Nathaniel had already begun.

Nathaniel sighed and pushed back his empty plate. "Well, I would not have expected this from my mother, I have to say."

Arabella smiled weakly. "She is not always placing you in uncomfortable positions?"

"Are you uncomfortable?"

What was she supposed to say? Arabella tried to collect her senses, now she and Nathaniel were alone together. She could at least be a little more direct, a little more honest than she might have been if his parents were in the room—or God forbid, her own.

Besides, had he not been honest with her? By the lake, when he had spoken of his hopes and dreams for a spouse. Had not Nathaniel revealed himself to be a romantic. A gentleman, in short, who was not disappointed with the result of the arranged matrimony itself, but the fact that the choice had been removed from him?

"Nathaniel," Arabella started softly. "Do you like me at all?"

It was clear he had not expected the question. Nathaniel's eyebrows shot up, and he opened his mouth twice without saying anything before he coughed and cleared his throat.

"What a direct young lady you are."

"Well, I think it only a fair question to ask at this point," Arabella said, forcing herself to be bold.

It was unlike her to speak so directly. True, she often wished to, and sometimes Arabella wished she could give in to that desire more often. This was far more her cousin Joy's approach to life, and Arabella knew she had it in her, if only she could release it.

But she was swiftly running out of options. Christmas Eve was tomorrow, and by Boxing Day, she would be returning in the carriage to London, to wait for her family's return from Chalcroft.

That left her three days. Three days to discover whether this arranged marriage was a complete mistake or something that, eventually, could be made to work.

"I have been here four days," Arabella persisted, speaking into the silence. "More than half my visit, Nathaniel, more than many people share in their courtship."

He snorted at that. "I would hardly call this a courtship."

"And whose fault is that?" Arabella said a little more sharply than she had intended.

Oh, the last thing she needed to do right now was offend him!

But thankfully, her boldness appeared to have endeared herself to him. At least, from what Arabella could see, Nathaniel smiled and settled himself a little more easily in his chair.

"That is true," he said quietly.

Heartened by his words, Arabella continued, "What many people share before engagement, or even marriage, could be as little as a few dances, a conversation at a card table, a walk in the park."

"You are a London girl."

She chuckled. "Yes. But you see my point. Many matches are made, good matches, which become happy marriages, without hours of conversation. Hours of conversation we could have shared during my visit here, but you have been far more interested in—in disappearing, and avoiding me, and not giving me…not giving *this* a chance."

Arabella drew breath at the end of her long speech and wondered whether she had gone too far. It was a rather bold pronouncement, but something in Nathaniel drew that from her.

He made her want to be bolder, to be more direct. To speak directly of what she wanted.

"And yet instead…" he said quietly.

Arabella sighed. "We have shared…what? Perhaps one pleasant conversation and one…one kiss."

A wry smile tugged at Nathaniel's mouth. "You did not like my kiss?"

Arabella's cheeks flushed scarlet. "What makes you say that?"

"Well, you describe the conversation as pleasant, but you give no descriptor of the kiss at all," he said in a teasing voice. Arabella could not tell whether this was his idea of flirtation or whether she was just being mocked. "You do not have any feedback for me? A scientist must collect data, you know."

Now heat was flooding through her entire body, and there was a strange buzzing in Arabella's ears which made it rather difficult to concentrate.

Feedback for Nathaniel, of his kiss? How on earth could she describe it when she was still trying to understand it herself?

This confusing gentleman, with his quietness and his aloofness, his penchant for dressing like a farmer and his interest in science…how was he at the same time so strange and yet so deliciously right?

"Well?" repeated Nathaniel, his gaze not leaving her, a strange intensity in his look that Arabella did not understand. "A gentleman's honor and pride are on the line here, Arabella, if you are still comfortable with me calling you that. Do you have nothing to say?"

Her chest was tight now, and Arabella found her hands clasped in her lap, the fingernails of one hand digging into the other's palm.

Because she knew what she wanted to say. What she mustn't say. What a lady of her breeding and social standing should not even be thinking, let alone saying.

Nathaniel sighed. "And I thought you were…something more. I was wrong."

Pushing his chair back, the man rose from his seat and stepped across the room to the door. He was leaving. He was leaving, Arabella thought in a panicked rush of heat, and he had not given her a proper chance to speak.

Without really knowing what she was doing, Arabella stood up so hastily her chair fell to the floor with a loud clatter. Her hands were still clasped together but her chest was heaving.

Nathaniel paused by the door and turned slowly to look at her.

Arabella stared at him. He was so handsome and so shy. And curious. And passionate. He was everything she wanted, and she was certain the more she learned of him, the more she would like. The more she would love.

She just had to give him this, show him just how committed she was to this arranged marriage.

"I liked the kiss," Arabella breathed.

Nathaniel raised an eyebrow. "Liked?"

"I liked it very much." Arabella swallowed, knowing she had to speak this, although she could barely breathe as she looked into Nathaniel's sky-blue eyes. "You…you made me feel wonderful. Warm. Warm all over."

Nathaniel's hand left the door handle and returned to his side as he took a step toward her. "And?"

Arabella hesitated, but this time the words came easier. Now the dam had been broken, her words could take flight. "And…and I liked how you held me. Your hands on my waist. And y-your tongue. Oh, Nathaniel, you could kiss me like that every day, and I would never tire of it. I would never tire of…of you."

He was closer now, though Arabella had not noticed him move. Her whole body was tingling, the mere memory of that kiss and her verbally recounting her emotions, her feelings, was enough to make her shiver.

Nathaniel lifted up her chin with his finger. "And?"

Arabella's breath caught in her throat. He was so handsome, so intoxicating. She would do anything he wanted, anything at all.

It was madness, and ridiculous, yet she knew it to be true. She was very close, dangerously close, to falling in love with him.

And he could see that, couldn't he? Nathaniel was no fool, he had proven that at the lakeside, by the swans. Surely, he could see the desperation with her.

"And I want you to do it again," Arabella breathed, her hands reaching out unconsciously, placing themselves on his chest. He was warm. She could feel his heart beating, faster surely than normal.

What did that mean? The wild thoughts scattered through Arabella's mind told her that he loved her, he hated her, he was aroused, he was disgusted—all these things and more.

Yet he said nothing.

After waiting for a few more heart stopping moments, Arabella wet her lips. "Well? What…what did you think of the kiss?"

Nathaniel said nothing but looked down at her. If Arabella was bold enough, she could lean forward and kiss him in turn. Show him what she wanted, what she needed. The longing in her was building so badly, Arabella thought she would burst with the anticipation.

And then he broke the silence. "I want to show you something."

CHAPTER SEVEN

"*I want to show you something.*"

For a moment, Arabella was not entirely sure she was going to obey the strange summons from the man who blew hot then cold with alarming regularity.

But his eyes…they were trusting. For the first time, Arabella was certain Nathaniel was not going to be sarcastic or wry, but earnest. Somehow, and she was not sure how—though the pounding in her heart suggested it was due to her scandalous honesty—she had managed to gain the trust of the future Lord Cartier.

"Arabella?" Nathaniel whispered her name, and Arabella shivered as his breath tingled on her skin.

Only then did she realize she had not actually replied. "Yes. Yes, show me."

A slow and slightly nervous smile crept across his face, and Nathaniel reached for her hand. His fingers were warm and strong, but Arabella was almost certain there was hesitancy there, too.

What did he want to show her? A shiver crept up her spine as she tried to consider what on earth it could be that Nathaniel wanted to show her—something that he evidently had not even considered revealing until his parents had gone.

Because they had gone. Arabella was vaguely aware of the

sound of a carriage pulling away from the drive. They were alone, she and Nathaniel, alone in Oxcaster Lacey.

She swallowed, her pulse flickering. What was she about to experience? Would she be pleased or repulsed?

Arabella swallowed. "Wh-Where…where are we going?"

Nathaniel smiled. "You would never be able to guess."

He moved, pulling her to the door, into the hallway. For a moment, heat flashed through her stomach to between her legs, Arabella was convinced he was going to take her up the staircase and to his bedchamber.

What would she do if that was what he wanted? If he wanted to make love to her, to show her perhaps what she was missing— or what she could enjoy every day once they were man and wife?

Almost dizzy with excitement at the idea, Arabella was only a little disappointed when Nathaniel dropped her hand by the front door—but only, it appeared, to help her into her pelisse.

"You'll need this," he said quietly, shrugging on his own mud-splattered greatcoat. "It is cold out there."

"Are we going to the lake?" Arabella asked hesitantly.

Nathaniel smiled. "You'll see."

His cagey remarks only increased her concerns as Arabella stepped into the cold afternoon air. Though it was only after luncheon, the sun was already dipping in the sky, heading back to the horizon. Its orangey glow reflected beautifully on the lake, flickering as the wind picked it up.

Arabella would have put money—if she had been a wagering sort of woman—on the thought that they were going toward the lake. It was, after all, the one place Nathaniel had appeared to be more comfortable. More himself. More able to be open with her and vulnerable.

Yet, although they did walk toward it at first, Nathaniel then took a turn to the left, toward some barns, which looked half abandoned. The estate could not need much additional income, Arabella could not help thinking, if they were not using the farms to their height. Why, Chalcroft was always attempting to get a little more funds from the land it owned. It had to.

But Nathaniel did not seem to notice the dilapidated state of the barns as they approached one in particular. There was a light in his eyes, a vibrant, brilliant excitement Arabella had never seen before.

No. No, that was not quite true. Arabella swallowed and felt a little glow of happiness. She had seen it once before—when he had kissed her. When he had taken her in his arms and bestowed a kiss on her lips.

Nathaniel halted when he reached the large barn door and looked at her with a strange expression on his face. "I…there are very few people who know about this."

Arabella nodded but could think of nothing to say. What on earth could be inside there? A boudoir, perhaps? Was this where he took his lovers when he wanted to ensure his parents had no idea he was bedding them?

A little fear crept around her heart. Was she about to be scandalized? Was Nathaniel thinking that she would so easily fall into his arms after all the rudeness he had treated her with?

"I will not ask you to swear to keep it a secret," Nathaniel said quietly. "I…I believe I can trust you, Arabella."

"You can," she said swiftly, squeezing his hand. She could barely feel her own, the freezing winter air taking all feeling from it, but she knew he felt the sensation.

Nathaniel nodded. "Well…here it is. This is the place that I go so often."

With his free hand, he reached out and pulled open the door.

For a moment, as Arabella released his hand and stepped into the warm barn, she thought Nathaniel had been playing a trick on her. It was…a barn. Haybales were all over the place, a few old pens left from lambing, perhaps. A few pitchforks were gathered in one corner along with what looked like a scythe, and there was a spare greatcoat hanging on a hook at the other end of the barn.

Arabella swallowed. Why on earth had he thought to bring her here?

But then something in one of the pens moved.

Arabella gasped, but instead of stepping away, she moved forward. Her eyes must have been lying to her—it was not possible that…

But it was. Arabella reached out her hands and carefully held onto the wooden fences that made up the pen and looked down at a beautiful, sleeping but gently stirring swan.

"The missing swan," she breathed.

She felt, rather than saw, Nathaniel's presence behind her.

"The missing swan," he repeated with a wry laugh. "Safe and sound, though a little damaged by the wintery weather."

Arabella could not believe it. Was this what Nathaniel had been doing all those times she had been looking for him? Hiding away in a barn, caring for a swan?

It did not make any sense. Why keep one here, why separate it out from its family? Even though she had been here but a few days, the Oxcaster Lacey lake did not look complete without its seven swans a swimming. It was why she had noticed it earlier.

"But…but why," Arabella breathed, looking at the majestic creature. Its features looked so soft, she was desperate to touch them—but not foolish enough to reach out a hand. "Why would you keep a swan in here?"

"I've not tamed it, nor captured it, if that is what you are thinking," said Nathaniel quietly.

Arabella saw the hurt on his face. She had injured him, though accidentally, that did not appear to matter. She had still pained him.

Only in that moment did Arabella realize, truly, what it meant to care for another. She had power over him, yes, but not merely the sensual power that she had felt rising up in her since the moment Nathaniel had kissed her.

No, it was more than that. Deeper. More mysterious.

Her words could injure him, even if she meant no harm, and that meant she had to be incredibly careful. Nathaniel's heart, she could see, was already partially in her keeping.

A sacred honor. She would have to be careful not to break it.

"I did not mean that," Arabella said gently. "I...I wondered what had happened for this situation to occur. For you to help."

Her words appeared to have mollified him, for Nathaniel flushed slightly with a smile.

"I am trying to help," he said with a dry laugh, "though I cannot help but feel I am drastically underqualified to do such a thing. Its wing, you see. It's damaged, I thought, if it was in here, safe, warm, not having to fly..."

Nathaniel's voice trailed away, embarrassment seeming to overpower him.

Arabella marveled at the change in him. It was difficult to believe this was the same man who had so proudly and so rudely informed her that he was not interested in the agreement their parents had made.

There was such complexity to this man, such depth. Arabella was not certain a lifetime would be sufficient to plumb them.

"All the birds here need a little help," Nathaniel was saying. "And I make sure that I come down here every few hours during the day to ensure they have enough food, water, that sort of thing."

Arabella nodded, but then his words caught up with her. "All of them?"

Nathaniel grinned. "You did not notice, did you?"

Arabella smiled, unable to help herself. "I did not. There are others?"

There were many others. Arabella could hardly believe she had missed them, but her eyes had been so taken with the flash of white weathers that she had walked straight past them.

She lingered along the pens now, Nathaniel by her side as he told her all about the different birds—and a few creatures—which had joined the others in this barn of wonders.

"And there—that's a barn owl, and you would think this was their natural habitat, but her wing never grew properly, I've had her for a few years now...hibernating wasn't an option, he couldn't get fat enough, so I keep him here…migrating I think, but lost their way, and they stayed together as a pair, so I wanted to care for them…"

The more they moved throughout the barn, the more animated Nathaniel became, creeping out of that cold and aloof shell he had retreated into the moment she had met him.

And Arabella understood—at least, she started to think she understood.

Nathaniel was shy. He was unaccustomed to company, let alone young ladies, and spent far more time here with the animals and birds that he cared for.

This was a part of himself, a part he had not thought he could share with another. Not even his parents knew, he told Arabella, though when she thought of the way that his mother had been concerned about his absence, she wondered whether he had underestimated the mistress of the Oxcaster Lacey.

"Here, look!" Nathaniel said eagerly, taking Arabella's hand once more and pulling her toward one end of the barn. "My fox! He had a broken leg when I found him, and the groundsmen were going to kill him, but I have managed to nurse him back to health."

Incredible pride radiated across his face, and Arabella was overwhelmed with a rush of affection.

Was this not precisely what she had wanted? To understand Nathaniel, to grow close to him, to share his life entirely?

"You have managed to nurse all these animals back to health?" Arabella asked as she meandered back to the swan. Of all the birds and beasts he had shown her, the swan was by far the prettiest.

Nathaniel looked a little abashed. "I mean, not all of them make it. I would greatly love to learn more, perhaps become an animal surgeon myself, but…"

His voice trailed away and his gaze fell. Arabella felt a prickle of sympathy for him. What on earth could have prevented a gentleman—one with means, a title, power—from doing something he wanted so desperately?

After all, it was not as though he was a woman.

"My parents," Nathaniel said simply. "They have no wish for me to have a profession, they consider it common."

Ah. Arabella sighed. Well, it would be a little radical for a gentleman with a title to go out in the fields and work with his hands. Had not she been astonished by Nathaniel's initial appearance, in the garb of a farmer? And that had been merely his clothes.

Could she honestly say she would have had no prejudice if she had known, before meeting him, that her future husband preferred laborer's work over sitting at tea?

"I see," said Arabella slowly. "So...so you never went up to university, then?"

Nathaniel shook his head. "My father said it was for second sons and gentlemen who had no fortune. No, a few of my friends at Eton went, but I returned here. I have been here almost ever since."

"You...you have not been to London then?" Arabella asked, attempting to remove the incredulity from her tones. It did not seem possible. Everyone went to London.

But now she thought about it... Nathaniel had not. Why else would she need to come here and visit, meet him for the first time? If he had always been in Town for the Season, they would have met countless times.

"No, I could not leave my creatures," Nathaniel said with a dry laugh. "You probably think I am a fool."

"Not in the slightest," Arabella said swiftly. Her hand was still clasped in his, and now they had been in the barn a length of time, her fingers had defrosted. She squeezed his hand with a smile. "Nathaniel, I...I am honored that you have been willing to show me all this. You do me a great honor by including me in your secret."

His smile was worth every word of praise she bestowed upon him, and more. Arabella shivered, conscious he would somehow feel her desire through the contact of their fingers.

But then, who could blame her? She had expected a cold, aloof, entitled—in both senses of the word—gentleman. One who would consider her beauty and her name and little else. She had been ready to try to build connections with a man with whom she was to spend the rest of her life, but for it to be difficult.

But Nathaniel…conjuring up feelings for Nathaniel was not difficult. It was a struggle to hold them at bay. He was kind, gentle, caring—far more caring than any gentleman she had ever met.

A little eccentric, perhaps, but what gentleman wasn't? He did not gamble or bet on the races or fight in back alleys—

And then Arabella began to laugh. How could she have been so foolish?

"What is it?" Nathaniel said, his smile faltering. "You…you are amused? I amuse you?"

Arabella nodded as she giggled, her laughter echoing around the barn. "Yes, but not about this. Well, sort of. Oh dear, you will think me so strange."

Nathaniel's shoulders relaxed. "I show you a barn of animals that I am secretly nursing back to health, and you think you are the strange one?"

"Well, you will have to be the judge of that," Arabella said with a smile.

Her gaze returned to the swan. Arabella wondered whether it was one of the parents, the pair who had been distant from each other but had eventually found each other.

They were separated now. Were they lonely? Did they feel the absence of their mate as keenly as Arabella knew she would feel the absence of Nathaniel once she was forced to return to London?

"What is it?" Nathaniel's voice was urgent, and Arabella could see she had not succeeded in calming him.

She sighed, a little embarrassment flushing her cheeks as she said, "Well, when I first arrived here, you were not…not as welcoming as you could have been."

Nathaniel laughed. "Understatement. Go on."

Arabella smiled. There was a connection between them now, one she could not have conceived of even a day ago—one she had no desire to lose.

She hesitated. Was she doing the right thing by revealing this?

But they could not enter into married life with these sorts of secrets, Arabella told herself. They needed to be able to be open, honest with each other…otherwise what was the point?

"Well, I was sure that you were keeping a secret," Arabella began.

"Which I was."

"But not the sort of secret I had guessed," she said.

"Dear God, what did you think I was doing?"

"It was not what I thought you were doing," Arabella said slowly, hardly knowing how she was brave enough to say this, but certain she was going to, "but who."

Nathaniel blinked, and Arabella flushed with a deeper heat. She had gone too far. A lady should not be saying such things, and certainly not to a lord!

But then he laughed. A low chuckle grew into a deep laugh, and Nathaniel grinned at her as he said, "My word, you believed I had a mistress somewhere on the grounds and was disappearing off to her!"

"I-I did!" said Arabella, hardly sure whether she should be pleased or panicked that Nathaniel was laughing.

Did he believe the whole idea nonsense—or was it actually true, and he was amused that she had finally found it out?

"You…you don't, do you?"

Nathaniel ceased laughing, though a smile still danced upon his lips. "Oh, Arabella. I have underestimated you."

"And I you," Arabella said honestly. "All of this, this barn, the way you care for birds and animals, your dreams to be an animal surgeon…I do not believe I could have ever guessed there were such depths to you."

She was surely not imagining it; perhaps it was the fading light. But no. Arabella watched as Nathaniel dropped his gaze, his cheeks flushed.

Was the great and previously aloof Lord Nathaniel Cartier...embarrassed?

"The truth is, I...I knew that it would be unlikely that someone else would...would understand," Nathaniel said in a low voice, so low that Arabella had to step forward to ensure she caught every word. "I could not believe that a young miss from London would ever sympathize with...with what I wanted from life. And you..."

Arabella's heart fluttered painfully in her chest, and she was suddenly very aware that they were still holding hands. Still connected. Even if it wasn't enough.

"You are so beautiful," Nathaniel breathed, looking up to meet her gaze with his light blue eyes. "So beautiful, Arabella, but more than that, you are witty and kind. I...I knew I would not be good enough for you, knew I would not impress, and you have confirmed that with every minute of your presence here."

Arabella's breath caught. Did he mean...

Nathaniel had been worried that he would not be enough for her? But she had spent the entire time since she had arrived here at Oxcaster Lacey worried that she would not be enough for him!

Had they both been circling each other, certain that they would not be able to make the other happy?

"You are...you are more than I had expected, and more than I deserve," Nathaniel said quietly, raising his free hand to stroke her cheek, then cup her face. "Arabella, I—"

She did not permit him to finish. Arabella knew what she wanted and could see in Nathaniel's eyes that he wanted it, too. This time, there was no hesitation.

Arabella leaned forward, used her free hand to grab the lapel of Nathaniel's great coat, pulled him toward her, and kissed him passionately on the mouth.

CHAPTER EIGHT

FOR A HEART-STOPPING moment, Arabella was not sure whether Nathaniel would recoil from her sudden kiss.

It was, after all, most unseemly for a lady to do such a thing. It was not expected for a lady to wish to kiss a gentleman quite so passionately …

It was simply not done.

That did not seem to matter. Nathaniel reacted instantly, pulling her closer, deepening the kiss, holding her tight against him, so tight, Arabella was not sure how they were managing to breathe.

This kiss continued far longer than their first. Arabella breathed him in, the warmth of the barn, the heady knowledge that Nathaniel had no mistress on the grounds that he was secretly meeting, allowed her to give more of herself than she ever had before.

Untamed, unrestrained, when the kiss finally ended, Arabella felt a little shaky on her feet.

"Well," said Nathaniel in a jagged voice. "That, I was not expecting."

Heat tinged Arabella's cheeks as she looked down at her feet. Of course, he had not.

A finger tilted her chin up so that she was looking into his face. Nathaniel was smiling wryly.

"I think if I had known there was such desire within you, Arabella Fitzroy," said Nathaniel quietly, "I would not have taken such a long time to be vulnerable before you."

Arabella smiled a little bashfully. "I have never— I have never done this with any other gentleman."

"I did not think that," he reassured her quietly.

"So, you must tell me if—if I…well, if I can do better."

Arabella felt the shame of her words across her cheeks, but she wanted to be honest with him. He was her first, the only man she had ever kissed.

It was natural, of course, that he would compare her to others he had kissed and find her in some areas wanting—but she was willing to learn, willing to be taught.

But as Arabella continued to gaze into Nathaniel's eyes, happy and warm in his arms, something about the way he was not quite meeting her gaze any longer made her hesitate. What…what was wrong? Why was he no longer willing to look at her?

"Nathaniel?" she said softly. "What is it?"

He laughed and shook his head. "I do not know how you have managed to get this idea in your head, Arabella—perhaps this mistress idea that you concocted has gone deeper into your mind than you had thought, but…"

Arabella's heart skipped a beat painfully. He was about to tell her something, something Nathaniel had kept from her until now, and it had something to do with a mistress. What was it? Did she not kiss as well as this woman? Was he disappointed in the way she shared her affection?

"What is it?" Arabella whispered. "You can tell me, Nathaniel. I promise."

Nathaniel sighed heavily as he tightened his grip around her waist. "You imagine me to be far more…more experienced than I actually am. That is all."

Arabella stared. He could not mean—surely Nathaniel could not be saying what she thought he meant?

They both chuckled as understanding dawned, and Arabella could not help but be amazed. Well, here she had been worried about disappointing the great and experienced Lord Nathaniel Cartier, when in fact…

"Nathaniel Cartier," she said in mock severity as Arabella pressed her palms against his chest, feeling his heart pattering under her fingertips, "are you telling me that…that I am your first kiss?"

"And well worth the wait, I can assure you," Nathaniel said in that low, teasing voice she adored so much. "I knew I was engaged to be married to you, Miss Arabella Fitzroy, and I knew that unless something drastic happened, such as our parents changing their minds—"

"Not very likely," Arabella agreed.

"—that you would be my wife one day," Nathaniel continued. "I did not wish to sully our future together by taking short term pleasure with another. I…I believed you would be worth the wait."

Arabella could not believe what she was hearing, but there was only the sound of truth in his voice.

He had kept himself for her. Despite surely many temptations and opportunities to lose his innocence, to take pleasure with another, he had not. He had waited.

Nathaniel glanced over her shoulder, and Arabella turned to see what he was looking at. The swan had fallen asleep, its head tucked under its wing. It was the most lovely creature Arabella had ever seen.

"We are like the swans," said Nathaniel quietly. "Two people destined to be together, but far away from each other for so long. Just because one's mate is far away, that does not mean you betray them for another. You wait. As I have waited for you."

Joy soared through Arabella's heart as she turned back to him. "I…I do not understand you, Nathaniel, but I think I am starting to. I am…I am honored by your attention."

"And by my affection," said Nathaniel seriously. "I hope you know that. I would not be…well, like this, here, if I did not admire and care for you."

Arabella smiled but did not reply with words. Her mouth, her kisses could easily share with him just how much she adored him in turn.

For she did. Despite all her fears about this visit, despite her frustrations with her father that he was sending her to Oxcaster Lacey over the Christmas season of all times, after all her confusion with Nathaniel, not understanding him, seeing him as aloof and irritating…

She knew him better now. She adored him. She loved him.

Impetuously, Arabella deepened the kiss, twisting her head to allow his tongue to meet her own. Frisson flickered through her body as they met, Nathaniel's desire for her instantly transforming into pleasure.

Arabella moaned. This was all she wanted. He was all that mattered.

It appeared he thought just the same. His hands had moved from her waist to her buttocks, and though before this very moment Arabella would have been terrified, astonished at the very thought that someone would wish to touch her there, with Nathaniel, it felt totally natural.

As though his hands belonged there. Almost as though every moment when he was not touching her was a moment wasted.

"Oh, Arabella," whispered Nathaniel as he pulled back from the kiss, his hair tousled, his eyes fierce with desire.

Arabella leaned forward, wanted to kiss him again, but this time he leaned back. She halted, a little ashamed of her blatant lust. The last thing she wished to do was lose his favor, not at this moment, when they finally understood each other.

"But—but I want you," she whispered, unable to help herself.

Nathaniel groaned and dipped his head, resting his forehead against hers. "You don't know what you do to me, Arabella."

In truth, she did. Arabella was no fool, she knew the…well, the mechanics of lovemaking. And she was not so lost in

Nathaniel's kisses that she could not feel the hardness of his manhood against her hip.

He wanted her. Wanted her badly, just as she wanted him, though there was no outward sign.

And that meant, Arabella thought wildly, that unless she said something, he would not know. He could not know just how much his desire for her was matched by her own.

Oh, if only she could find the words, if only she could reveal to him the thoughts rushing through her mind—the desire she had for him. Images, hopes, and tumbled desires mingled in Arabella's mind so fervently that she was not sure she had the ability to do anything about it.

But she must try. She had to explain to him, had to reveal her thoughts.

Arabella swallowed. "You do it to me, too. I-I want you, Nathaniel. I want you to make love to me."

For a moment, the words hung in the air, echoing in Arabella's mind. She could hardly believe she had spoken so immodestly and out loud.

But if there was anyone in the world who could be told that innermost thought, it was Nathaniel. Arabella felt safe in his arms, but also in danger—in danger of losing herself entirely to the lust rushing through her veins.

Nathaniel was staring at her as though he had not heard her correctly. "You…you want me to make love to you?"

Hardly able to breathe, Arabella slipped one of her hands over his heart down his chest, lower, and lower, until Nathaniel gasped and shuddered. Her fingers had scraped over the bulge of his manhood in his breeches. Then he groaned as she stroked the fabric gently again, feeling the pulse of his desire.

"I want you," Arabella whispered, not looking away from him. "All of you. Everything you are, Nathaniel, I w-want it. I want you. Do you…do you understand?"

She hoped he did, hoped he would not reject her. It had taken all her self-control to continue with this, and Arabella knew if

Nathaniel turned her away, she could not bear it. The ache within her that only Nathaniel created was starting to hurt, and she needed him, needed him to help her ease it.

Nathaniel breathed heavily, as though only just able to control himself. "My parents are out. Gone for the night. And we are engaged to be married, you know."

It took a moment for Arabella to realize what Nathaniel was trying to say, and even then, she needed to hear him say it properly. Say it aloud.

"What do you mean?"

Nathaniel kissed her hard on the mouth. "I mean I want to make love to you. Let me, Arabella. I want...I want to explore it with you."

Unconsciously, Arabella's hand tightened around Nathaniel's manhood, and he groaned and stepped away from her, breaking the connection.

"Come with me," he said, his voice jagged, as though he barely had enough breath to speak. "Come on."

Arabella took his offered hand and found herself pulled, out of the barn, across the parkland, around Oxcaster Lacey to a side door she had never spotted before, though that was no great surprise. The place was a maze.

With every step, her heart beat faster and her excitement grew. Just what she had agreed to, Arabella knew was scandalous. Young ladies did not give themselves up for lovemaking before they had been wed in church. Had been raised to know that, to value the innocence she would give to her husband on their wedding night.

But was this not, in a way, her wedding night? Nathaniel had admitted his affection for her, even if he had not said the words precisely as she had expected, and he had said himself, they would be married.

"My parents are out. Gone for the night. And we are engaged to be married, you know."

They were engaged to be married—they would be married

soon if Arabella had anything to do with it. So why not experience those sweet pleasures that were only to be shared by a man and wife? Why not submit themselves to the desire rushing through their bodies, the desires they could no longer contain?

The side door opened onto a corridor Arabella did not recognize, but that did not matter. Nathaniel knew. He pulled her down the corridor and opened a part of the wall, which was a door in disguise, to reveal a staircase.

"A hangover from the days when priests had to be rushed out of homes," he said breathlessly as he pulled her up the steps, one after another. "Come on, Arabella—I am not going too fast for you?"

Arabella answered in the only way she knew how. She stopped, pushed Nathaniel against the wall in the staircase, and kissed him.

Nathaniel moaned under her possessive touch, her hands pushed back his jacket, forcing it to the floor. Arabella could not think what had taken over her, but all she knew was that she needed him, needed to be as close to him as possible—and clothes were merely getting in the way.

And he responded in kind, giving her the confidence she needed to be sure that he desired her just as much as she desired him. They stood there, Nathaniel's back against the wall as Arabella leaned into him, kissing for goodness knows how long.

Eventually Nathaniel groaned and pulled away from her. "Damnit, Arabella, why do you have to be so delectable?"

She flushed at his words. She had never considered herself...well, anything like that. With five sisters, there was always someone else taking the attention of the room.

But this was her moment, her man, her chance to experience the devotion of a gentleman, and she was not going to forget a single second of it.

"Come on," Nathaniel said, pulling her up the final few steps. "This way."

Arabella nodded, eyes hazy with desire, hardly able to know

how she could walk, but managing it all the same.

They had come out onto a corridor. Perhaps near the family bedchambers, she thought wildly as Nathaniel pulled her along it—but when he opened a door and pulled her inside, the hazy late afternoon sunlight drifting through the window, it was onto a room that Arabella could not believe was Nathaniel's.

Though it was handsome enough, it had none of the grandeur of her suite. There was not much furniture in here, save a four-poster bed that looked magnificent; but there were no chairs, no bedside tables, no chest of drawers, no looking glasses or toilette.

"Where are we?" Arabella whispered as Nathaniel let go of her hand to close the door.

She was not entirely sure why she was whispering; it did not appear that anyone else was in this wing of the house, and as Oxcaster Lacey was so large, she was certain her voice would not carry.

Nathaniel leaned against the door, smiling wryly. "Guest bedchamber. I was not sure I could prevent myself from removing all your clothes if I had to get to the other side of the house, to my own."

Arabella flushed. It was the first time she had really heard much of Nathaniel's own desire, and it was strange, wonderful, to hear the hunger in his voice.

He wanted her. He desired her. He wanted to take all her clothes off.

A small moment of hesitancy fluttered across her mind. Was she ready for such a thing, for such intimacy? Was she ready to lose her innocence, right now, today?

Nathaniel must have seen the concern in her eyes. "We do not have to—"

"I want to," said Arabella swiftly. She did. There was no true fear in her heart, only anticipation she had for a second considered fear.

But she trusted Nathaniel, knew that they were fated to be

together. This arranged marriage, she had thought it was pulling her away from her life—but it was quite the opposite. It was pulling her toward it.

Nathaniel was her life.

He smiled, a little unsure himself. "I…well, I am sure there are gentlemen out there in the world who have done this before, who…who know what they are doing. They would surely give you a better experience than I would."

And there he was. The Nathaniel she knew and loved. Arabella could not believe she had thought him aloof and irritating when she had first met him, when she could see now that all it was, was fear.

Nathaniel had feared intimacy, feared meeting someone he would be forced to wed, feared disappointing them.

But she knew now he could never disappoint her.

"This is all new to me, too," Arabella said softly. "And I-I am glad. I am glad we are sharing this together."

Nathaniel stepped across the room and pulled her into his arms, kissing her furiously, pouring all his fear into his passion.

Arabella welcomed it, welcomed him. She clung to him, kissing him just as eagerly. Her body tingled with the pleasure he washed through her, and she moaned a little as his kisses trailed down her neck toward her breasts.

"Do…do we need to be quiet here?" Arabella managed to gasp.

Nathaniel kissed her collarbone, making her quiver. "No, there are no servants in this part of the house, and it's so old, no sound ever reaches the living quarters. We can be as unrestrained as we want."

"Oh, God," Arabella moaned, unable to hold it in any longer. "Then kiss me, Nathaniel, love me!"

His fingers scrabbled to the buttons down the side of her gown, and Arabella returned the favor, pulling at the cravat which had been tied most untidily. As the fabric fell to the floor, as she kicked off her shoes and pulled down her stockings,

Arabella gasped. Her gown was undone. The only thing holding it up now was her arms.

Nathaniel looked at her, half afraid, half passionate.

Arabella smiled and, knowing not how this surge of confidence had overcome her, allowed her gown to fall.

He groaned aloud. "Arabella, you are so beautiful."

Beautiful. She had never believed such a thing until this moment. Arabella flushed, looking down at her body, now only covered by a light undershift. Perhaps it was beautiful; but she was certain she would like it all the more once Nathaniel had touched it. Kissed it. Made love to it.

"Now you," Arabella said, her throat a little dry.

Her fingers hardly managed to undo the buttons that went down Nathaniel's waistcoat, and by the time it and his jacket was removed, she was so filled with desire, so unable to concentrate as Nathaniel's lips once again met hers, that she simply pulled the shirt over his head in desperation. Arabella did not care.

Her fingers traced the lines of his chest, the muscles she had felt but never seen, the hair that had tantalized her at the top of his chest, which she now saw coated most of it, trailing down to…

Arabella swallowed. His breeches.

"Now you," Nathaniel murmured.

With slightly shaking fingers, she lifted the straps of her undershift off her shoulders, pulled them out, and allowed it to fall.

She stood there, utterly naked, but Arabella felt no shame. Shame was for when one was doing something wrong, and this was not wrong. This was right. So right.

Nathaniel looked, slightly abashed, but clearly desperate to take in every inch of her. She watched as his gaze lingered at her breasts, the curls of her secret place, the way her hips flared.

"Christ," was all he could manage.

Arabella laughed slightly, a rush of power searing through her heart. It was pleasant, rather heady, to have such power over a man. To know he was so enamored with her.

"Now…now you," she managed to say.

It took Nathaniel less than a heartbeat to pull off his boots and pull down his breeches.

Arabella gasped. He was not wearing anything underneath.

She was not entirely sure what she had thought gentlemen had on under their breeches, but she had assumed it was something. Perhaps other gentleman did.

But not Nathaniel. There he stood, in all his glory. The hardness she had felt through the fabric of the breeches was there now, for her to see, erect and desperate for her touch.

Arabella could feel that, knew it instinctively. Before either of them could say a word, she had reached out and touched it.

Nathaniel shuddered. "Careful, or this will all be over very quickly."

She did not understand. Why would it be over? What could prevent—and then Arabella's understanding caught up with her, and she flushed.

"Come with me," she said softly, her hand moving from his manhood to slip into his own hand. "Love me."

Nathaniel did not need much more of an invitation. As Arabella moved to the bed, he suddenly lifted her up and placed her upon it, covering her body with his own.

Arabella gasped in his mouth as Nathaniel kissed her, kissed her hard, the intensity of the moment tenfold as his chest pressed against her breasts. There was something about being skin to skin, of nothing being between them, no barriers, nothing to keep them apart.

"I waited for you, for so long," Nathaniel murmured as his kisses meandered down her neck and along her collarbone. Arabella arched her back, needing more, not sure how to ask for what she wanted. "So long, and you were so worth it, Arabella, dear God…"

"Yes, yes," she murmured, her lashes fluttering, her body hardly able to take in images, the pleasure of his mouth was so intoxicating. "I—oh, Nathaniel!"

Nathaniel had grazed one of her nipples with his mouth, the roughness of his beard causing snaps of pleasure to crackle along her body.

Arabella gasped with the pleasure of it all. A moment of ecstasy, only a moment, but a teasing hint of what was to come.

"Do that again," she begged, arching her back, trying to bring her breast closer to his mouth. "Again."

Nathaniel obliged, this time taking her nipple into his mouth hesitantly, then with more certainty as he felt her reaction. "Like this?"

Arabella shuddered as his tongue twisted around her nipple, teasing it in one direction and then the other, and she cried out his name as his hands met her hips, holding her in place.

Her hands were in his hair, then gripping his shoulders as though she would fly off the face of the world if she did not hold onto him. Arabella did not know how she could endure any more pleasure, and yet she wanted it, wanted more, wanted everything. Everything he could give her.

She had not consciously moved this way, but Nathaniel was now lying between her legs, his hard, throbbing manhood pressed against her hip, and she could feel it quiver, knew what he wanted.

Knew what pleasure she could give him.

In a sudden moment, Arabella twisted on the bed and tipped Nathaniel over so that she lay over him, straddling him.

"What are you—"

"Hush," Arabella said, placing a finger on his lips and glorying in the look of him. Surely there could be no greater man than Nathaniel; he was majestic. Every inch of him made her quiver and want to do something wild.

And so, she did. Creeping down his body slowly, kissing each inch of him she passed, exalting in the way he shuddered and gasped her name as she nipped and kissed, Arabella finally made it down to his manhood.

It was slightly intimidating, she had to admit. Never having touched one before, Arabella was not entirely sure that what she was doing was right, but instinct drove her.

Slowly, ever so slowly, Arabella lowered her head, her breasts grazing Nathaniel's thighs, and kissed the very tip of his manhood.

"Arabella!"

Nathaniel's instant reaction, the way he spoke her name, told Arabella everything she needed to know. With greater and greater confidence, Arabella kissed and licked that most intimate part of him, grateful to be given such access, knowing no one had ever touched him like this, kissed him like this, licked him like this.

When she finally took as much of him as she could into his mouth, Nathaniel's hand grabbed her head and entwined it in her hair, his whole body quivering.

"No—no, stop."

Arabella immediately removed her mouth from him, the soft sweetness that she was starting to enjoy, and looked up in fear. "Did—did I hurt you? Did I do something wrong?"

She so wanted to give him pleasure, to show him just how much pleasure he had given her, that fear started to replace wonder in her heart—but one look at Nathaniel's face told her that she had done nothing wrong.

"It's not that," Nathaniel panted, a wry smile across his face. "It's just—for our first time, I want to be inside you. Do you understand?"

Arabella nodded and twisted off him to lie beside him. Without a word passing between them, Nathaniel moved to nestle between her legs, as he had done before—but this time, he was a little lower down. His manhood was right there, by her secret place.

She looked up into his eyes and saw the fear, saw the hesitation in Nathaniel's face.

"I trust you," Arabella whispered. "I want this."

Nathaniel groaned as he sank into her, and Arabella whimpered—but not from pain.

The pain she had expected did not come. Instead, there was merely the sensation of stretching, almost immediately followed by a twinge of pleasure. Then a second, deeper, growing, and Nathaniel pulled back and sheathed himself into her once again, and Arabella gripped his shoulders and moaned with pleasure.

"That feels so good," she murmured, lifting her lips to be kissed, which Nathaniel swiftly obliged. "More—faster."

"Deeper," groaned Nathaniel, leaning on his elbows as he tried to control the pace and the depth. "Oh, yes."

Arabella abandoned herself to the intimacy, to the sensations, to her body, which knew what she wanted, what she needed.

Nathaniel thrust into her harder now, deepening the pleasure, building the ache within her to a point that Arabella was not sure she could bear any more. This was it, this was everything, this was the moment she had craved without knowing it, and it was building, building, his right hand now teasing her nipple, squeezing her breast, and Arabella could not bear it!

"Nathaniel!" she screamed, her body exploding with pleasure, the crest soaring over her, every inch of her body pouring with ecstasy.

Arabella managed to look up and saw Nathaniel's face contort with pleasure as he suddenly thrust into her hard, several times, without a single pause.

"Arabella!"

And then he collapsed into her arms.

Arabella held him, held the man she loved. Held the man who would be everything to her from this moment on. Held the men she would never let go again. Her perfect mate. Her swan.

CHAPTER NINE

I F ARABELLA COULD have flown down the staircase, she would have.

Everything in Oxcaster Lacey appeared to be…glittering. Everything was golden, all things she looked at were perfect, exactly how they should be.

Arabella's heart soared as she looked around the great hall. This was her home—her future home. Everything she had feared, everything she had felt to be wrong, or out of reach…she had achieved.

"I waited for you, for so long. So long, and you were so worth it, Arabella, dear God…"

She shivered, despite the warmth of the great hall, with its large fireplace blazing. She had never considered such a connection possible. In her limited understanding of the loving act, she had always heard far more about what the gentleman did, what the gentleman experienced—almost to the point where she had believed, unconsciously, that the entire thing was for him.

But Nathaniel had proven that wrong. He had been—oh, so loving. More than she could have hoped. More than she could have dreamed.

And the last two evenings, no matter what the servants saw, Arabella and Nathaniel did not go to their separate bedchambers after dining and talking with his parents in the respectable drawing room.

Oh, no.

Once the wall sconces had been dimmed, and the rest of the household of Oxcaster Lacey had gone to sleep, a figure had crept out of her bedchamber, down the corridor, and into Lord Nathaniel Cartier's.

To receive the lovemaking of her life.

Arabella shivered, heat flushing her cheeks. It was scandalous really—and yet, not so scandalous. Why should they not enjoy each other, taste each other, fill each other? Why not explore the heights of happiness, the depths of pleasure, the ways a man and a woman could enjoy each other?

They would be married soon, that was certain, was it not? Therefore, why not begin to enjoy the fruits of that marriage, now?

Arabella smiled wistfully to herself. Three perfect days. Days spent in conversation and helping Nathaniel with a few of the birds and animals he cared for in the barn. Evenings filled with hilarious whispered conversations, desperately hoping his parents did not hear, Arabella's heart thumping wildly at the very thought of being overheard or understood.

And nights…

Nights filled with passion. Arabella had never known herself to be so attracted to another, nor so desired in return.

And Nathaniel was a quick learner. Arabella's stomach lurched as she thought of the way he had kissed her last night, kissed her all over.

He may never have been with another woman before her, but she had been with no gentleman. They had learned together, eager to please, eager to pleasure, and Arabella was finding herself wishing away the days so that they could reach the nights…

But she must not think of that now. Arabella shook her head slightly, as though that would enable her to rid her mind of the delicious memories.

Today was Boxing Day. Her last day.

A twist of her heart pained her, and Arabella found herself lifting a hand to her chest, as though that would stop the agony.

Leaving here—leaving Nathaniel? It was strange to think how dearly she had wished for it when she had first arrived, when she had not understood Nathaniel, nor he, her. She had longed to leave then, to escape what had felt like a dreary festive season—but now Arabella could not think of leaving him without very real pain.

How long would it be before she was able to see him again? Weeks? A month, even?

There had been talk, before she had left London, of the Cartiers coming to London for Easter—but could she wait that long?

Arabella smiled wistfully as she gazed into the fire. And today she had managed to make her way downstairs to the great hall, in the full knowledge of where the breakfast room was.

She had done it. Despite her fears at the beginning of her stay here, she had managed to conquer Oxcaster Lacey. Conquer her objections. Conquer Nathaniel's heart.

"There you are!"

Arabella turned with a bright smile to the gentleman who had descended the staircase.

Nathaniel. Hair wild, as usual, with his blue eyes sparkling and that ridiculous smock. Arabella could not help but laugh to herself. There were some things about Nathaniel that she knew it would be pointless to attempt to change; they were who he was, like the swans and the animals and the barn.

That smock was one of them. He truly was a strange lord indeed.

Nathaniel stepped toward her, pulled her into his arms, and kissed Arabella so deeply, that she whimpered slightly in his embrace, clutching him to her, desperate for it to continue. Thought was not necessary at the moment.

When they finally broke apart, Arabella was breathless and more than a little eager to return right upstairs and enjoy some slow, gentle, early morning love making.

"Arabella," Nathaniel whispered.

"Yes?"

"I—"

"There you two are, and—oh."

Arabella and Nathaniel sprang apart as they saw Lady Cartier emerge from the breakfast room, a napkin in her hand and a rather pink expression on her face.

Heat rushed to Arabella's cheeks, and she dropped her gaze immediately. Oh, this was uncomfortable! Being caught kissing Nathaniel, and by his mother no less! She could well imagine the awkwardness if they had been discovered by her mother!

But Nathaniel did not appear uncomfortable at all. On the contrary, he slipped his arm around Arabella before he spoke.

"Good morning, Mother," he said cheerfully. "Starting without us?"

"Waiting for you," said Lady Cartier a little sternly, but there was a small smile appearing now on her lips. "Come on."

Arabella glanced up at Nathaniel, half afraid she would be censored when she entered there for making a display of herself. Why, if the mistress of the house happened upon them, what were the chances that a servant could do the same?

Lord Cartier was already seated at the breakfast table, this time on the corner nearest his wife. This meant that as Nathaniel sat down, Arabella found herself seated at a right angle to him. Closer to him. More conscious of his gaze on her.

Partly to distract herself than anything else, Arabella reached for the teapot. That was it, tea. She could surely return to being a completely normal and calm person, perfectly designed for Society, if she could just have some tea.

The steaming hot liquid poured into the cup, and Nathaniel leaned over and dropped a slice of lemon in it.

Arabella looked up in surprise.

Nathaniel grinned. "I do pay attention, you know. I know you prefer a slice of lemon in your tea. I know many of your preferences."

Heat seared her cheeks, and Arabella looked down, hoping his parents had not heard him. That was the thing about Nathaniel. She was particularly good at underestimating him; had done from the very beginning when she had first arrived here, and it appeared she was still doing so.

How was it that Nathaniel was able to watch her so carefully, lovingly see what she wanted, what she desired, then immediately move to give her what that was?

Perhaps that was just the way he loved. Arabella had seen it with the creatures he cared for in the barn, the way that he went above and beyond to look after them, even though he had no training.

It was the way he expressed his love, Arabella told herself, trying to prevent her heart from pitter-pattering in her chest. He may not have said it aloud, with words, but this was how he spoke of it. By caring.

Far more than any other gentleman she had ever met.

"Do try not to hide behind your newspaper, dear," said Lady Cartier sharply.

Though her words were technically a suggestion, their sharp tone made it perfectly clear to Arabella that Lord Cartier was being given an order.

And he had rather hidden behind it, raising it up over his face so that all Arabella could see were a few pages discussing the stock market, something terribly dull.

"Hmmmph," came the only sound from Lord Cartier.

Nathaniel winked at Arabella, who tried not to giggle.

What sort of things would they argue about, Arabella could not help but wonder, her mind daydreaming as Nathaniel politely asked after the Spensers, whom his parents had so recently visited.

"Very well, I thank you, son. Indeed, I thought Lady Spenser much improved since we…"

Perhaps they would eventually argue over the smock, Arabella thought wistfully, sipping her tea, which was wonderfully lemony, and watching Nathaniel humor his mother. Perhaps one day she would tire of it and demand that it be gone.

Or perhaps, and the thought was a rather startling one, perhaps Nathaniel would find habits of hers irritating. The thought had never occurred to her before, but Arabella supposed one always thought one's own habits were perfectly natural and not at all objectionable.

She considered for a moment what those irritating habits of hers could be. She could not think of a single one.

Well, Arabella thought with a smile as she sipped her tea, she was certain that Nathaniel would be able to find them out for her. Over time. They would grow more alike, she was certain, as she believed her own parents had done. With time. With love and affection.

If there was one thing that Arabella was absolutely certain she would never tire of, it was Nathaniel's interest in the natural world.

How could she even countenance attempting to squash Nathaniel's greatest passion, his deepest interest?

No, to the contrary. Arabella had already started to concoct ideas about encouraging Nathaniel's interest in science and nature. Would it be possible for a gentleman a little more advanced in years than most university men to attend Oxford or Cambridge?

Or perhaps, was there an animal surgeon who could be prevailed upon to come and live here at Oxcaster Lacey, teach Nathaniel all that he wished to know?

Whatever would make him happiest, Arabella thought wistfully as she watched him speak kindly to his mother, his eyes bright, his face alive with joy in a way she had rarely seen.

That was her aim, now. She had found the man she wanted to marry, wanted to spend the rest of her life with—and she would spend that life trying to make it better for him. Make him happier.

"—Miss Fitzroy?"

Arabella blinked. Both Nathaniel and his mother were looking at her expectantly, as though she had been part of the conversation. They seemed utterly unaware she had spent the last five minutes daydreaming about her future husband—which, she thought hastily, was probably no bad thing.

"I beg your pardon?" she said a little meekly.

Nathaniel snorted. Lady Cartier gave him a look.

"I *said*, Miss Fitzroy," said Lady Cartier a little sternly, "that I am glad you and my son are getting along a little better, after…after the slightly bumpy beginning."

It was Arabella's turn to laugh this time. Bumpy beginning was an understatement. Why, she had been utterly convinced halfway through her visit that there was no point in even attempting for the wedding to go ahead!

But that was all different now. Arabella could not fathom a world in which she and Nathaniel were not wed. In fact, it was hard to remember at times that they were not man and wife yet.

Not that she was about to admit that to his parents, of course…

"Yes, it is rather a relief," Arabella said brightly, trying not to catch Nathaniel's eye. "I had thought things may be a little tricky, but I had not imagined his lordship to be quite so difficult."

"And neither had I imagined Miss Fitzroy to be quite so beautiful," cut in Nathaniel with a wry smile Arabella could not help but notice out of the corner of her eye. "What a relief, eh, Mother?"

Arabella could not help but laugh, and then laugh all the harder at Lady Cartier's astonished expression. Well, really! Nathaniel was such a tease. She was going to have to get accustomed to his cheek, for she was certain that she would swiftly become the brunt of it at times.

What a relief that she knew him to be kind and gentle under all that gruffness and brashness. Nathaniel was just shy, a man who had not spent enough time with others to understand how brusque at times he could really be.

But she would learn. A rush of affection soared through Arabella as she looked at him, the man she knew she loved. She would learn, and he would learn. They would learn together.

"Now, do not tease me, Nathaniel," said Lady Cartier reproachfully. "You know your father and I have had high hopes for this arranged marriage for many years, haven't we, Cartier?"

"What?" said Lord Cartier's voice from the other side of the newspaper.

Arabella could not help but giggle. To think she had felt awkward with the Cartiers when she had first arrived! It was impossible to imagine now.

And very soon, they would be. Her own family, at least. Arabella was determined, the moment she returned to London and her family returned from Chalcroft, to ask her father about a special license.

Why wait? Why wait for the rest of her life to begin when she was absolutely sure she knew what she wanted it to be?

"Well Mother, I am not sure whether you could have chosen a better partner for me," Nathaniel was saying, making Arabella flush. "No, truly."

He reached out a hand, and Arabella, feeling a little warm to do such a thing before his parents' eyes, took it. His fingers were warm, encircled in hers. She could feel his pulse—or was that her own? It was hard to tell.

"I had thought myself quite of a different nature to Miss Fitzroy, but that was before I knew her," Nathaniel said, his voice falling into seriousness for the first time that morning. "But I was wrong. We are quite the same."

Arabella could not help but smile. "Birds of a feather flock together."

A footman entered holding a silver tray, upon it lying one single envelope. He stepped around the table to stand by Lord Cartier and cleared his throat.

"What?" asked Lord Cartier, still behind the raised newspaper, which was laid down most bad-temperedly. "Ah, the post."

"I still do not understand," said Lady Cartier as her husband ripped open the letter without much thought for the seal and started reading. "What has all this got to do with birds?"

"Swans," said Arabella with a mischievous smile at Nathaniel. He raised an eyebrow, almost as a warning sign, but there was such a delicious smile on his face that Arabella felt confident enough to continue. "We would like them, at the wedding."

"The—the swans?"

"The seven here," Arabella said boldly, her hand safely in Nathaniel's.

Oh, was this what it was to be married? To know the support of your spouse is just there, waiting in the wings to encourage you whenever needed? To know that no matter what happened, they would be there, carrying you, loving you?

"Well, whatever game it is you two are playing, I hope you have joy of it," said Lady Cartier, a little put out, but she smiled nonetheless. "It does my heart good to see you so affectionate with—"

Lord Cartier cleared his throat impressively. "Before you continue, my dear, I think it only right to read you this letter I have just received."

Arabella was astonished to see a rather severe look on his face. She had never seen the man so serious.

"What is it?" asked his wife, clearly struck by the lack of levity in his tones.

"It is a letter," said Lord Cartier impressively, "from Mr. Arthur Fitzroy."

Now the entire table looked at her. Arabella frowned slightly. She could not think of a reason why her father would be writing to Lord Cartier—if he had anything to say, would he not be writing to her?

And then a horrible memory circled back into her mind. The letter. The letter she had written to her Papa.

She had not posted it—she had left it on her desk in the suite when she had seen Nathaniel walking around the lake.

But she had not seen the letter since. Was it possible…dear Lord, was it possible that someone had gone into her suite, seen the letter, addressed, sealed, ready for the post…and taken it upon themselves to post it?

Heart in her mouth, trembling slightly at the thought of what this reply from her Papa could contain, Arabella had no time to open her mouth and cease Lord Cartier's reading of it.

"'My dear Lord Cartier,' your father writes," said Lord Cartier stiffly. "'I regret to inform you that I have received a letter from my daughter, Miss Arabella Fitzroy, stating her distaste for the match we made for our children so many years ago.'"

Arabella swallowed, but her mouth was dry. This was a nightmare—this was precisely what she did not want! How could she stop him?

Nathaniel's hand slipped from her grasp.

"'It pains me to hear that my daughter's arrival has not been met with greater joy and welcome,'" Lord Cartier continued to read from the letter. "'My daughter's happiness, as you can imagine, is of the utmost importance to me. Though I had wished for this match to be fruitful, it is clear that we cannot force either of our children into such an arrangement.'"

No, no, this could not be happening. Arabella's lungs had constricted, preventing her from taking deep breaths, deep breaths she sorely needed.

How could this have gone so wrong, so quickly? Mere moments ago, they had been laughing, her hand in Nathaniel's, knowing she was going to be wed to the very best man she ever knew.

Now that was all falling apart. Because of her own stupidity, because of her rush to tell her father how unhappy she was, she was about to lose everything.

Arabella looked at Nathaniel, who was resolutely not looking at her. He looked…as though the world had ended. As though he had been told he would be locked in a cage, never to be let out into nature.

As though he had been betrayed by the person he trusted the most.

"'I must therefore consider this arrangement of marriage between my daughter Miss Arabella Fitzroy and your son, Lord Nathaniel Cartier, to be at an end,'" finished Lord Cartier, reading the final words from the letter in his hand. "'This engagement is cancelled. It is over. Send me back my daughter.'"

CHAPTER TEN

THE WORDS ECHOED around the room, around Arabella's head, forcing her to hear them over and over again, a curse, a death knell, causing her very heart to stop.

"I must therefore consider this arrangement of marriage between my daughter Miss Arabella Fitzroy and your son, Lord Nathaniel Cartier, to be at an end."

This was a nightmare. Arabella was certain she had accidentally fallen into a nightmare and would, at any moment surely, awake to find herself safe and sound, in her bed. Preferably with Nathaniel by her side.

But it was not happening. No matter how many times she blinked, ragged breath drawn into her lungs, Arabella could see only the same scene before her eyes.

The breakfast table, covered in a white linen cloth and a teapot, several cups, a stack of toast, marmalade, two hard boiled eggs that were cooked every morning and no one touched, and the abandoned newspaper.

Lord Cartier and Lady Cartier, staring, eyes wide, confusion on her face and disappointment on his.

And the other occupant of the table, the one whose opinion mattered so much to Arabella and yet she had hurt so badly.

Nathaniel. He sat there, face drawn, closed, the pain she had caused him forcing him to pull away from her, she could feel it.

Arabella could sense the distance between them.

He had trusted her. He had trusted her not only with his body but with his heart, a far more delicate thing, and in his eyes, she could see that she had betrayed him.

"This is all new to me, too. And I-I am glad. I am glad we are sharing this together."

Arabella swallowed, tasting the bile in her throat, and knew she could not make the words be unsaid, no matter how much she wished it. She could not make the letter her father wrote unwritten, nor take back the words that she herself had written in the original letter—a letter she had never intended to be sent.

I know you and Lord Cartier made the match with the best of intentions, but you could not have known just how abominable that man—I will not call him a gentleman—is.

So please, Papa. Write soon, and tell me that I am forgiven, and that the whole thing will be called off.

She closed her eyes, hands shaking, and opened them again, but there they all were. Waiting for her to respond.

As though she could respond to such a thing. As though there was a way she could defend herself, herself and her father, for betraying their trust.

Arabella opened her eyes and glanced at Nathaniel, hoping he could see by the look of shock and upset on her face that she was as surprised by her father's words as he was; that she had never intended such a thing; that such a pronouncement came against her wishes.

But Nathaniel would not look at her. His gaze had fallen to his hands resting on the table, seemingly unable to meet her gaze. Unable or unwilling, Arabella did not know.

She swallowed, tasting the bitterness in her throat, and reached forward with one of her hands to take his own.

Nathaniel moved his hand away.

Panic rushed through Arabella's veins. If only his parents were not here, she could explain to him, could be honest and say she had feared the arranged marriage had been a mistake—

before…before everything!

Before they had talked. Before she had grown to know him, before he had revealed himself to her, been vulnerable.

Before they had shared the most important thing that two people could ever share.

Arabella knew she had to do something, knew this painfully silent moment could not continue forever.

Knew if she did not do something and soon and right, then the love she had found—for it was love, she was certain of it—would be lost. And she would regret, for the rest of her life, the loss of such a perfect affection. Such an adoring partner.

The swan of her heart, the perfect mate who had been far away but had been found.

As guilt tinged her heart, for Arabella knew all too well that it was her own hand which had condemned Nathaniel in her father's eyes, she wished heartily she had never sat down to write that dratted letter.

But that could not be changed, not now. She had to face what was before her, deal with the situation she found herself in—or lose the man she loved.

"Nathaniel," Arabella said urgently in a low voice. He did not look up. "Nathaniel, I—"

"Nathaniel Cartier, you have let us both down!" Lord Cartier rose to his feet, though he did not need to for his words to be impressively loud.

It may have been Arabella's imagination, but she believed the china on the table rattled slightly at Lord Cartier's words. His glare was most alarming, and Arabella turned instinctively to his wife to calm the situation—but she, too, had risen to her feet.

"We should have known you would not manage to secure Miss Fitzroy's heart," said Lady Cartier with none of the anger and far more sadness than her husband. "Oh, Nathaniel, we should not have permitted you to speak with her alone, what have you said to her?"

"You did not tell her about…about your obsession with nature, did you?" Lord Cartier glared at his son, and Arabella's heart prickled painfully as she watched Nathaniel look resolutely at his hands in his lap. "Boring that poor girl to tears, no wonder she has no wish to marry you!"

On and on they went, a tirade of disappointment, and Arabella could not think what to do. She was in their home, their guest; it was not her responsibility nor her duty to interfere. And Nathaniel was their son, albeit a grown one.

But it was torture. Every word from their mouths dripped with disdain and frustration, all with the assumption that as soon as Arabella had started to get to know their son, she had immediately decided the man wasn't enough for her.

Wasn't…wasn't enough?

Arabella could think of nothing more incorrect. If anything, she had been burdened for the last few days with the panic that Nathaniel would wake up one morning, take a look at her, and realize that he could certainly do far better.

She swallowed, feeling the tension in her shoulders, unsure how to make Lord and Lady Cartier halt berating their son—but as Arabella's gaze shot over to Nathaniel, she saw precisely what she had to do.

"Stop."

Arabella could hear her own heartbeat in her ears, a rush of blood soaring through her, making her feel powerful. Was that why she had stood to her feet?

Lord Cartier opened his mouth, but no sound came out as Arabella glared at him, her hands clenching the table as though somehow that would make it easier to do what need to be done. Say what needed to be said.

Lady Cartier wordlessly reached for her husband's sleeve and tugged it. Very slowly, he sat down.

The two of them were staring at her, as though they had never seen a young lady speak her mind before.

Perhaps they had not, Arabella found herself thinking wryly, trying not to smile. After all, they only had a son, and it did not appear as though they had many visitors. Nathaniel certainly had no idea what to do with her when she had first arrived.

"Miss…Miss Fitzroy," Lady Cartier managed to say, her voice shaking—though with anger at her, or her son, Arabella could not tell. "You do not seem to understand—your father—"

"My father is my own problem, and I will deal with him when I return to London," Arabella said impressively, power rushing through her.

She had no idea where it was coming from—her love for Nathaniel perhaps, her passion for him, her determination to be with him, no matter the cost.

Because she loved him. Knew she could not be without him. Knew that after all their fears that they would not be acceptable to the other, they were in fact perfectly suited.

Matched. Designed to be mated for life.

And nothing, not her own father, not Nathaniel's parents, was going to come between them. She was determined.

"This is all your fault," hissed Lord Cartier toward his son.

Nathaniel opened his mouth, but Arabella spoke before he could. "How dare you speak to Nathaniel like that!"

Lord Cartier stared at her, pink splotches of anger rising in his cheeks. Arabella could see she had offended him but could not stop, could not permit anyone to speak to Nathaniel like that.

How dare he! How dare anyone speak harshly to a man who had done nothing but care for living things for his entire life?

"Nathaniel Cartier is a great man," she told the stunned Lord and Lady Cartier. "How dare you criticize him for seemingly not enchanting me—when he has done far more than that!"

"Arabella…" Nathaniel muttered under his breath, still not looking at her.

But she did not heed him. She knew what he was concerned about, that she would reveal that they had tasted of each other's delights before they had been wed.

But that was not what Arabella had meant, and she continued on, fire rushing through her body, her temper finally matching her red hair.

"This gentleman was not someone that I immediately understood," Arabella said in a clear voice, reaching for Nathaniel's hand. She found it, somehow, she did not know how. "I believed him proud, arrogant, unruly, and utterly disinterested in both me and a marriage match."

"I thought you were supposed to be defending me?" muttered Nathaniel.

Arabella could not help but smile. She looked at him, the man she would give everything up for, the man she was defending proudly, and saw a twitch of a smile on his face as he met her gaze.

"I have grown to understand him now," said Arabella in a softer voice. She was hardly aware of what Nathaniel's parents were looking at now. She was more interested in looking at Nathaniel. At the man who had captured her heart. The man whose conversation was surprising and unusual and who had been honest with her.

And loved her. She knew that, though the words had not been said. He loved her, loved her entirely. As she was.

"I must defend him, for he will not defend himself," said Arabella quietly. "Nathaniel was unsure of me, and I of him. The marriage had been arranged long before we could even be conscious of such a thing, and we had little information of each other. We did not know—we could not know whether this arrangement would be a success."

"But the birds, the animals!"

Arabella looked at Lord Cartier, who had spluttered those words. "And what of them?"

"You must admit, my dear," said Lady Cartier in a low voice. "It is not…not usual for a gentleman, let alone a man of rank and title, to have found such an interest. It does not…worry you?"

Arabella stared. "How could it worry me that the man I wish to marry cares deeply? That he sees pain and wants to halt it, sees injury and wants to cure it? You think that would make me *less* likely to care for him?"

Nathaniel's hand squeezed her own, and Arabella took heart from it. He did care for her, even after her father's letter cast a shadow of a doubt over her own affections.

"A gentleman who wishes to bring healing to the world is one to treasure, not censure," Arabella said passionately. "I do not understand you at all! Why did you not permit him to study, to take his innate skills far beyond what they are? I see Nathaniel, and I see a man who is already so much more than any other man I have ever met, and I…I love him."

She swallowed as she spoke, but the last few words escaped her lips. And really, they should have done before, days before.

The moment she had known she had fallen deeply in love with Lord Nathaniel Cartier.

The moment she had known she could not live without him. That this arranged marriage, though it had started in a strange way, was everything she wanted now in the world.

But she could not entirely wipe out the stain of the letter from everyone's memory.

"But your father's letter is quite clear," said Lord Cartier, picking it up and glancing at it. "'This engagement is cancelled. It is over. Send me back my daughter.' What say you to that?"

Arabella took a deep breath. If she had not been so hasty as to write the letter in the first place, then she would not have found herself in this mess—but as it was a mess of her own making, there was only one thing for it, as Nathaniel would say.

To unmake it.

"I wrote to my father halfway through my visit to Oxcaster Lacey," Arabella said as calmly as she could manage, tightening her grip on Nathaniel's hand as though terrified he would attempt to escape her. "I was…I was lonely. I was afraid. Nathaniel and I had not yet spoken from the heart. We had not managed to understand each other."

"A fault that was entirely my own," Nathaniel said in a low voice.

"Not at all," Arabella said. "I think we both bear the blame there. I was too quick to judge, too swift to see the smock and the dirt, and not the man underneath."

A grin crept across Nathaniel's mouth. "That you were."

"And so, I wrote a letter for my father, but I did not post it," Arabella said, emphasizing the last few words. "And between writing that letter and returning to my room, Nathaniel and I had…had an encounter. By the lakeside, as we watched the swans."

Heat rushed to her cheeks as Arabella remembered that moment. The first conversation they had had which had been open; when Nathaniel had revealed his fears about their arranged marriage; when they had discussed the swans, the story of how they had found each other; and their very first kiss…

"Are you prepared, Arabella, for what might happen if you do seduce me?"

"And when I returned to my suite, I had absolutely no thoughts of sending that letter to my father—in truth, I had entirely forgotten I had written it," admitted Arabella, a shiver of pleasure rushing through her body at the mere recollection of the delicious kiss. "It was posted on my behalf, however, so I bear the responsibility for leaving it out."

"But then," said Lady Cartier, "you did ask your father to end the arrangement!"

She needed to make it clear to them, could not permit them to think she had any doubts now.

"Lord and Lady Cartier, I…I love your son," Arabella said quietly, not looking away from Nathaniel's gaze. He stared, unblinking, back at her. "I love him. I love Nathaniel, and because of, not in spite of the way that he cares for birds and animals. I love how that speaks of his qualities of tender care, and scientific curiosity, and a desire to do good in the world. How…how could I not love him?"

She hoped Nathaniel understood her. Did he? Did Nathaniel see the devotion in her face? Could he hear it in her words?

For Arabella knew if she was not able to convince them, all three of them, that her words were true, then the arranged marriage she had been irritated by only a few weeks ago would be taken from her—and it would be as a death to lose him.

"Well!" Lord Cartier rose to his feet. "I think this is something that can be made right, Miss Fitzroy, if you are determined to have him."

Arabella's heart leapt. "You...you do?"

"It takes a special lady to see our son in that light," said Lady Cartier, rising to her feet as she spoke, not unkindly. "Come, Cartier. Let us leave these two—we have a letter to write to Mr. Fitzroy, and I believe it will take the efforts of both of us."

Arabella did not look around as they left the breakfast room, Lord Cartier rather slamming the door behind them. She was far too interested in Nathaniel.

He was still seated, still had her hand in his, and was still looking at her; but there was silence on his lips. He said nothing, and Arabella stood there, feeling tension rise in her neck, painfully sparking across her head, as she felt the weight of the moment.

After her declarations of love and admiration for him...he had said nothing. Was Nathaniel truly hurt by her father's letter, by the letter which she had written which had been sent to him at Chalcroft, even if she had not intended it?

Was there too much hurt there? Would Nathaniel find it impossible to forgive her, impossible to see past the pain she had caused?

Was—and the thought seared through her heart painfully, burning it, contracting it—the marriage planned between them at an end, despite his parents' wishes to reinstate it?

Despite her love of him?

"Do...do you really mean that?"

Arabella blinked. She could not think what he meant, but there was a look of desperation on Nathaniel's face, as though he needed to know the truth before he could even think of the future.

"What do you mean?" Arabella whispered.

She had intended so speak more strongly, but she could not. All the breath had been taken out of her by her defense of Nathaniel to his parents.

In a rush, Nathaniel rose from his seat, pulled Arabella's hand, and twisted her around as she stumbled forward. Before she knew it, Arabella was pressed up against the wall of the breakfast room, Nathaniel's hands on either side of her as he leaned against the wall, against her, breathing heavily.

"I need to know," he growled, light blue eyes not leaving hers. "I need to know if you meant it. What you said about me. About how you…you admired me. About how you loved me."

Arabella's heart was fluttering painfully, but it quickened as she saw what he was asking.

Nathaniel needed to hear it again, hear it when they were alone, when they could be truly open. He doubted himself, even now, doubted that anyone could care for him.

"I cannot believe it," Nathaniel said jerkily, removing one hand from the wall to cup her cheek, to stroke her face, his fingers brushing across her lips. "That a woman like you—so beautiful, so elegant, so thoughtful, far quicker than I had ever imagined, far wittier than anyone I have ever met…that a woman like you could look at me, and l-love me…"

"I love you, Nathaniel," Arabella whispered, gazing deep into his eyes. "I love you, for all of you. For the gentleman with a title, for the man in the smock who cares for swans, for the delicious man who took me to his bed—"

By that point, the temptation was too much for both of them and Nathaniel crushed his lips against hers, worshipping her mouth, teasing pleasure from her that made Arabella shiver against the wall, made her cling to him.

Nathaniel broke the kiss, leaning his forehead against hers. "I…I never thought I would be so desperate to hear those words."

"I never thought I would be so regretful of a letter I never meant to send," whispered Arabella ruefully. She could feel

Nathaniel's heart beating rapidly "I am sorry, Nathaniel. Can you forgive me?"

Arabella was not entirely sure what she had expected as a response to her words of apology; she had hoped, naturally, for its acceptance, or perhaps a further discussion, if necessary, of just how remorseful she was.

What she did not expect was a mischievous look that she had never seen before.

"What?" she asked.

Nathaniel's grin widened. "My parents think we are arguing in here—at least, I am sure that is what they think. And they have their letter to write to your father, begging him to accept me as a son-in-law."

"Well," flushed Arabella, wondering what on earth her Papa would think when he received that letter. "What of it?"

A wicked glint appeared in Nathaniel's eyes before he kissed her delicately on the mouth. "Well, that means that they are going to leave us to our own devices for a little while. More than enough time for me to show you just how much I forgive you."

Arabella's eyes widened. "What…what do you mean?"

Nathaniel did not answer, at least, not in words. He kissed her once more, deeply, his tongue demanding entrance, and she gave it to him the moment she felt his tongue tracing the lines of her lips.

And then she gasped in his mouth, her cry of surprise absorbed into his groan of delight as Nathaniel's hand pulled up her skirts as she leaned against the wall.

"Try to be quiet," Nathaniel groaned as he kissed her neck, Arabella's eyelashes fluttering shut as she felt the instant twinges of pleasure that he gave her when he did that. "Try, Arabella."

"I can be quiet," Arabella gasped, hardly knowing what she was agreeing to. "I can—Nathaniel!"

He caught her lips with his own to keep her quiet as she cried out his name, but thankfully the household clearly thought they could be arguing, so they were not interrupted.

Arabella whimpered in the kiss. Arguing? They were doing precisely the opposite of arguing, and she could not understand how Nathaniel knew precisely what to do with his fingers as they slipped inside her, inside her secret place, and she was warm and wet and welcoming him, stretching to allow him deeper, and deeper…

"Christ, Arabella, you feel wonderful," panted Nathaniel. He was obviously finding it as difficult as she was to keep quiet, as his fingers slowly teased and stroked.

"Nathaniel," whimpered Arabella, her eyes shut to best experience the intensity of his caresses.

Arabella moaned as Nathaniel's mouth trailed kisses down her neck, her whole body arching to feel him deeper, to plunge his fingers further within her, and then she whimpered his name again and again as his questing mouth descended to her breasts, capturing her nipple through her chemise and gown.

"Nathaniel, Nathaniel, don't stop…"

"Arabella, come for me, come for me," he whispered between nibbling at her breasts, first one and then the other, starting the beginning of the ecstasy Arabella knew only he could give her.

For here it was—the fire, building between her legs, as his fingers stroked her into submission, and Arabella clutched at his shoulders as the wave overcome her, and she could not help but cry out his name just as his lips returned to hers.

"Nathaniel!"

The pleasure rocked her body, thrusting her between Nathaniel and the wall, and Arabella gave herself up to it, abandoning all sense of control for the ecstasy.

Arabella was not entirely sure how long she had been standing there, held up against the wall by Nathaniel's strong arms. All thoughts of quiet had disappeared from her mind, impossible, but Nathaniel's lips had captured most of her moans. When her eyelashes fluttered open, it was to see Nathaniel grinning, desire pooling in his eyes.

"Dear God, I love you," he breathed. "I have loved you the moment I kissed you the first time."

"I love you," Arabella said breathlessly, clinging onto him, determined never to be parted from him. "I will always love you, always love your kisses."

A smile crept across Nathaniel's face. "My parents will still be writing that letter. Why don't we go upstairs, and you can show me just how much you like my kisses."

Arabella nodded, hardly able to believe this was her life, her love. After years and miles apart, the two swans had found each other. Would mate for life.

"Only," and Arabella flushed as she spoke the words she had thought but never believed would have the courage to say, "only if you do that again. But with…with your tongue."

Nathaniel kissed her swiftly and hard. "I always will. Every day of your life—and especially at Christmas. The time when we first met, first fell in love, and knew we would be happy."

"Happy," echoed Arabella, joy rushing through her. "Happy, forever. Mated, for life."

About Emily E K Murdoch

If you love falling in love, then you've come to the right place.

I am a historian and writer and have a varied career to date: from examining medieval manuscripts to designing museum exhibitions, to working as a researcher for the BBC to working for the National Trust.

My books range from England 1050 to Texas 1848, and I can't wait for you to fall in love with my heroes and heroines!

Follow me on twitter and instagram @emilyekmurdoch, find me on facebook at facebook.com/theemilyekmurdoch, and read my blog at www.emilyekmurdoch.com.